Loving A Boss

A Hot Girl Summer Story

Pen N Paper

Table of Contents

Best-selling author Pen N Paper delivers again with *Loving A Boss: A Hot Girl Summer Story*

It's a hot girl summer for best friends, Magic and Eureka. They know all about having a good time, hyping up one another, doing them. Magic is a single mother between jobs. She is tired of the up and downs with her baby daddy Tom Tom. Used to him spoiling her and paying all the bills, she has some decisions to make after he gets locked up yet again. Magic needs a come up and fast. The bills are piling up, so she takes a job at one of the hottest new soul food restaurants in town. She struggles with mixing business and pleasure with her new boss Avant.

Eureka is Magic's ride or die friend. She is single with no children and lives above her means. She loves to have fun and live carefree and encourages Magic to do the same. It's her idea for the two to have a "Hot Girl Summer". She has two men who want her love and have important decisions to make while running around being a hot girl.

Avant owns the hottest new soul food restaurant around, Belle's Kitchen. As a businessman who is no stranger to the streets, he puts a lot of time into his business neglecting his love life. Against his better judgment, he hires Magic and they seem to have a thing for one another. There is just one problem, his bitter baby mama insists that she wants that old thing back so she refuses to let him go.

The summer is too hot and life is too short to live with regrets! Live your best life, love on a boss and have a hot girl summer

Chapter 1 Magic

It's about 88 °and the temperature is rising. It is too hot for the fuck shit. Muthafuckas can't wait for it to get hot to show out. This summer its going down on the books for us. I'm going be on my Hot Girl Summer shit. In case you're probably wondering just what the hell that means, its simple as it can get. Hot Girl Summer is all about living your best life and acting up like on your best or worst behavior depending on who you ask.

See me I'm a Hot Girl. I'm going step. I'm going to do what I want because I am that bitch. I stand ten toes down on that and I don't take no shit off anyone. These other chicks can have that coldest winter ever mess, right now it's my time, it's my summer!!!

As much as I try to keep my cool, it's always some bullshit. I was sick and tired of being sick and tired. My best bitch, Eureka sat her big fine ass at the table slathering cream cheese on her bagel without a care in the world while sipping on her mug of coffee. This bitch meant she was going to eat a meal or make herself at home anytime she came over here. She needed to be putting in on the groceries the way she ate over here.

"So what are you going to do?" Her voice was country but she had the attitude of a city girl.

A stack of unpaid bills were lined up on the table. I may as well had laid my damn edges right there with them because I was going to snatch all of them bitches out trying to get my mind right! I needed money like yesterday.

I shrugged my shoulders as I stood at the sink. "Guess I'mma look for a job. These damn bills are piling up around here. Tom Tom keeps calling me. I gotta get some money! That nigga act like it comes from out the sky."

I had a country ass voice too. We were both born and bred in the Commonwealth of Virginia, where the wealth was not common but we was going get to it by any means necessary. I was over a whole lot of shit and at my wit's end. I didn't know how much more of my nigga or this bill situation shit I could deal with.

Eureka popped her lips and started grabbing invisible air, clicking her long colorful nails. Hood bitch finest, my girl didn't care what came out of her mouth. "Girl screw him. He has a roof over his head. Let's try to keep one over yours. I just want me a big dick, rich nigga. He needs to have plenty money, a nice house, nice cars and just getting to the money. I'm trying to be loving on a rich ass nigga! And last but not least he needs to be spending that shit and breaking bread with me. You need to get on board and get you one. Bitch it's a hot girl summer!"

I rolled my eyes. I was trying to figure out how I was going make ends meet and she was over here with her little hood dreams.

"Well, it's not like I'm going find his ass today so be realistic."

Eureka had read one too many urban books, this bitch had worked up her own Prada Plan.

"Well since you not down with the plan to find you a rich nigga," Eureka replied, pouring way too much of my sugar and cream into the steaming black mug of coffee, "that new restaurant by the salon is hiring and you don't need experience. They need cooks, servers, waitresses, bartenders and all that like yesterday. I'm 'bout to be living my best life though. You better fuck with me."

I was trying to do some shit on my own without loving on a rich nigga. Loving on a nigga for his money and all that he could do for me was the reason I was in this predicament now. It was time for me to just get a job. My best friend was always on her best shit and today was no different.

Eureka whipped a menu out of her purse with the manager's number written across the top in big red letters. She had a chance to try out the menu before the place even opened yet due to its close proximity to her job.

I looked at her like she was crazy. "Bitch you know I don't have experience doing shit but being a bad bitch!"

"You are the one who keeps saying you need a job. Well, I guess you better use that experience and call them. Shit being fine should count for something. Good as you look being a waitress shouldn't be too bad or too hard."

I scratched my head. "The way my attitude is set up, girl I don't know."

"Bitch the way your bills set up I do know."

She slid me the menu across the table. My money was getting really low just like my patience so I said fuck it and called to set up the interview with the manager as my best friend looked at me like a proud mother. A bitch was all smiles when the manager told me to be there within the next hour for an interview.

Dragging around in my favorite, ugly robe and house shoes I needed to get a move on if I wanted to make it there on time.

"Oh shit. Let me hurry up. We have to be there soon." I was excited. This was the best news all week.

"Go get dressed – business appropriate, not club attire, but practical. I know we on our hot girl shit but not right now- and I'll drive you over there!" Eureka quipped.

I rolled my eyes at her. I didn't have no gas in my car I was definitely going to take her up on the offer but first I had to talk my shit.

"Says the same one wearing catsuits and fishnets to do hair! Girl, I got this."

She made sure to mention for me dress appropriately because she knows how I love to dress provocative and sexy even though it would cause fights and arguments with my baby daddy Tom Tom. That nigga was jealous as hell when it came to me.

With no time to spare I raced upstairs and began dressing. I threw on a black pencil skirt and some pumps with a six-inch heel. I opted to go bare legged with no stockings, unless they were fishnets I was not about to put that shit on anyway. I kept the white, button up blouse strategically open, allowing a glimpse of my black lace bra to show, pushing my titties up. I brushed my coarse, natural hair until it laid perfectly in place, making sure to use the spoolie to hit them edges and baby hairs just right. Popping my glossed lips, I smiled in satisfaction for getting dressed so quickly. My smile would have dazzled even a blind man. I looked the fuck good!

I was nervous. This was technically my first job interview! The butterflies in my stomach were doing the Wobble!

When we arrived at the restaurant I couldn't believe how nice it was. A crew was installing a new sign in the window and true indeed the place was right next to the salon where Eureka worked. Eureka stopped talking to whoever the nigga was she was telling lies to on the phone to wish me luck before I got out the car.

I walked up the sidewalk to meet with the manager and those same butterflies from earlier were still making my stomach flutter. Entering the dining area, I was not greeted by the manager I had spoken with over the phone, which surprised me. I would soon find out he was the owner, Avant Anderson.

"Hello. You must be Magic. Call me Avant, I'm the owner." He extended his strong, ringless hand for a firm handshake. "I'm sorry but the manager Patron had to leave at short notice so I'll be conducting the interview."

My palms were sweaty. I felt my stomach flutter again, but for an entirely different reason. This man was fine as fuck. He was tall, light skin with hypnotic dark eyes and close cut hair. His expensive charcoal grey suit appeared to be tailored and fit his body to perfection. Even his shoes looked like they cost a bag. I was very glad I'd dressed the way I did.

He looked over the resume that I had threw together in under twenty minutes as we talked informally at one of the white-clothed tables in the corner away from the other staff. The restaurant would not open until noon but the workers shuffled around handling business. This place was definitely going to be a busy establishment. As much as I wanted to give this nigga my undivided attention I found it very hard to concentrate. He man impressed me so much as I sat across from him with my legs crossed as I embellished my work history.

I have customer service experience, *yes I had collected money for my man.*

I have experience with money, *I counted it up for my man.*

I have serving experience, *I've served a few fiends for my man.*

I have restaurant experience, *I've dined in many establishments.*

Truth is, I had never worked a day in my life. My man Tom Tom was the one always taking care of me. I had never done an honest days work in my life and I hoped that this fine motherfucker sitting across from me couldn't tell that I was lying. Shit, I didn't even have a real resume, this was some shit I had copied off the web and tweaked. I was just going with the flow.

Still nervous, I knocked the glass of water over that one of the servers brought to the table over on the bogus ass resume I had made.

"No need to be nervous beautiful."

I laughed nervously.

"Someone will get that don't worry about it." Avant signaled one of his staff to come over and clean the spill. "So where was I?" He wiped the resume off with a cloth napkin and continued telling me about his plans for the restaurant and his expectations.

I hung on to his every word. I was certain that I had come across as a babbling idiot, as I was anxious to get the job. I was looking forward to getting this job so I could work around him every day. It was silly, I know, but my body was aching for him. It had been months since I had some dick up in me.

I was over here planning to make him my work bae and had no clue as to whether or not I'd even get the damn job until he reached across the table and took my hand and asked if I could start tomorrow. I was shaking, his big strong hand covered mine and Avant noticed and looked at me with concern.

“What's wrong Magic?” he asked with concern in his voice. “Are you feeling aight? Are you sure you have what it takes for this position?”

I nodded my head, feeling silly. “It's nothing!” I lied. “I can handle any position.” I raised my eyebrows.

Now that was not a lie. He didn’t need to know what I was really thinking as I crossed my legs tightly to keep my composure.

“Please tell me,” he repeated with kindness.

I sighed. “I am glad I got the job - and thank you for that - but since the minute I laid eyes on you, I thought you were one of the finest men I've ever seen. Damn...” feeling every inch the fool, and knowing I probably lost my chance at employment I stopped myself.

He laughed, but it wasn't a cruel or mocking laugh. “I thought you were sexy yourself.” He licked his thick, full lips.

I smiled, but this smile was not a shy one. “What do you mean though? I think I am sexy all the time. That’ not a thought, that’s a fact.”

Avant looked me over. I knew he liked what was before him.

"I think we need to talk a little more in depth in my office."

He looked down the hallway. When he stood up, I followed as he led the way down the hall away from the kitchen. He locked the door and sat down behind his desk as I stood close by.

"Is anyone coming in the office anytime soon?" I leaned closer to him. I needed to know what the hell I was about to get myself into. Avant shook his head and I flashed him a dazzling smile.

"No. You have me all to yourself for the moment." He undid his neck tie.

"Okay then!"

I stepped away from him and began to unbutton my blouse in front of him. Shimmying out of my shirt, it fell in a puddle to the floor. I now stood before him in stilettos and underwear. This man was going to be my bae and my boss! My legs felt like jelly underneath me, but I was determined to have this nigga!

"Damn you thick." He marveled at my fat ass that was not too big and not too small. It was just right.

I came to his chest at five, six with thick legs, and a nice ass to waist ratio with brown sun kissed, skin the color of the darkest maple syrup I was just as sweet. I loved everything about my body. It was something about that brown skin that always drove all the niggas crazy. My long, 4C natural hair had never been relaxed and I had it up on a high bun. My round pretty face held a smile as I waited for whatever was about to come. I was never one to wear too much make up but I had my eyebrows micro bladed so they were arched perfectly. My nose was pointed and not too wide or stubby like a button. It fit my face perfectly and I wore a small good hoop on the left side. My lips were large and soft but again they fit my face too.

I loved all of this melanin. If I didn't know anything black was beautiful and I owned that shit. My white, square teeth would have been perfect had I gotten the braces my grandma wanted me to get but since I didn't I had a very small gap that most people overlooked. Right now Avant looked at me like I was the best thing he had ever saw in his life as I stood before him.

I bet he never thought he'd be ready to fuck someone he was about to hire in his office this morning when he got up. The way I smiled, the way my hips swayed seductively as I walked towards him, the sparkle in my eyes and my shining, full lips I knew that he was turned the fuck on. I was about to put this pussy on him so good.

I looked at the bulge in his pants. I knew he had a big dick and I couldn't wait to feel him up in my sugar walls. It had been like eight months since I had some dick so I was about to enjoy this.

I crushed my full lips against his. His lips felt like velvet clouds as they pressed against mine. I hadn't been kissed like that in forever. I wanted to taste him inside and out as my tongue slid across his lips, and he tensed. I wanted it all! My fingers stroked his cheek feeling his neat facial hair as we kissed, my big titties pressed tightly against his strong, muscular chest. He still had on way too many clothes since the only thing he had removed was his tie and his shoes.

"Let's get you out of that silly suit!" I purred suggestively undoing his buttons.

"Silly? Baby this Gucci is very expensive," he joked.

"That's irrelevant and a waste of money when you're going to be naked and fucking me!" I was feeling cocky as I pulled on his shirt to help him out of his clothes.

There was a desire in me that was overtaking all of my inhibitions. I could tell from the bulge in his pants that Avant had a big dick and that he knew how to fuck - I wanted to ride it, to have him fuck me doggy style, to just beat down my walls, and to pump in and out of my pussy, until I couldn't come anymore. I wanted him to take me to the old town road as I rode until I couldn't anymore!

Yep. Avant was feeling me too as I pulled him towards me again. I kissed him and raked my coffin shaped nails onto his now exposed back. He let out a sharp groan that thrilled me and made my clit jump. I smiled in satisfaction as I felt him shudder with pleasure. He stumbled slightly as he removed his slacks, standing before me, his new employee, nearly naked.

Running my palm flat against his enormous, dick I had to compliment him.

"Nice."

I pulled it completely out of his boxers and began to caress it, feeling every vein and pulse, wanting to take it in my mouth, wanting to drain him and make him beg me for more. I couldn't help but to drop to my knees and lick and slurp around the head for a second, teasing him.

After teasing him we made our way over towards the leather couch.

Why the fuck did he have a couch in the office anyway?

Aggressively, I pushed him down and made my way back between his legs. I seductively smiled down at him and slid off his boxers. His dick was huge - I didn't know if I could take all of his dick - but I wanted to try! I was determined to have as much of Avant Anderson in me as I could take!

Getting it nice and wet, I took him in my mouth. I wasn't quiet about loving this job as I sucked, slurped and gasped for more, wanting mouthful after mouthful of his anaconda. He ran his fingers through my hair, playing with my bun as I gobbled him. Occasional moans of pleasure escaped his lips. I know I was making his toes curl the way I was deep throating his big dick. Stopping, I swung around and straddled his face in a 69 position. He had brought out the freak in me had me thinking I was a damn acrobat or gymnast stretching my body like this.

Avant wasn't hesitant for a second about eating my, fat, pretty, bald pussy. Even with brown skin, I had pink, pretty, full pussy lips. He nibbled and licked and tongued my hot slit until we were mutually moaning. I know my kitty smelled fresh and sweet and he wanted to stay there all day, taking in all of my sweet nectar, as he licked me deeper, tasting my juices on his stiff tongue.

Matching each other's lust in nearly perfect unison, I licked, he licked. He sucked, I sucked. I was coming all in his mouth and he sucked it all up. I needed every bit of this release.

"Ohhhhhhh yes, baby!" I almost cried as I fucked his mouth with my pussy. My last orgasm left me weak as hell. All I could do was lay back and smile. He rubbed over my body and smiled.

After I gathered myself, I could wait no more. I was ready for my next orgasm from his pole. I climbed aboard his large dick and thrust myself upon it. Considering his size I should have lowered myself slowly on him but I wanted to feel every inch, every vein. He pushed up making sure to put every inch in me. I bounced up and down, riding him, finding a rhythm as he fucked me back.

His hands played gently with my pierced tits as I rode him, tightening my pussy muscles around his shaft, milking as much pleasure from it as I possibly could.

"Ohhh god, Avant, you have good dick! Fuck me, fuck me hard with that big hard dick!" I yelled out boldly, tightening my pussy, driving him crazy. I didn't give a fuck who heard me as I went to work on him.

I bounced up and down on Avant's big, black dick and he matched my every movement. He would shove deep into me, hearing my little "oooh, oooh, oooh's" of lust and my singsong "*fuckmefuckmefuckme*". His groans immediately followed, and our bodies slapped together in an erotic dance.

I swirled and wiggled my hips, rolling them in an erotic motion, then slamming against him again. Our bodies were hot and sweaty as my pussy pulsated around his massive meat. Harder and harder, faster and faster, we fucked in his office.

During my job interview.

I had to let him know that I was a hard worker.

Pumping, thrusting, moving together in unison until neither could wait anymore.

Finally, with a shared scream, we both exploded. Avant came inside my tight pussy, my juices mingling with his come. I slid a finger down there and licked it clean, leering a little at him.

"I think this job will work out for us both Magic!" Avant smiled as we both cleaned up.

"Yes, it will!" I ran my hands over his chest.

I walked out of the office looking like I had just been fucked well and rode hard. I was no longer nervous or fidgety as I walked out of the office, towards the car where Eureka waited for me. The server who greeted me when I walked in earlier smiled at me like she knew a secret.

Could she hear me moaning and screaming?

"So, when do you start?" The girl asked as she continued to put salt and pepper shakers on the table.

Careful with my words I said, "I start tomorrow. I can't wait." I wasn't sure who she was to Avant so I didn't want to say too much.

I guess she was reading my mind. "Welcome aboard. You're going to like it. Avant is my brother."

"Well, that's great. What's your name?"

She knew what we had been doing. I could tell by the smirk on her face. "Ava is my name. It looks like you made the cut. Let me get back to work." She laughed and walked away.

Before our private, in depth conversation, I learned that Avant had to finish the interviews because the manager Patron had to leave early. Good thing for me that I met with him instead. I was in need of a good piece of dick and a job. He also confirmed that he was looking for beautiful, friendly staff to work for him, someone like myself. All smiles I made my way to Eureka's car satisfied that he picked me to do the job.

A little on the plus size but not quite the BBW, Eureka sat in the car with the air on full blast listening to NBA Young Boy. She jumped when I pulled the door handle.

"What the hell you jumping for? Scary ass!" I kicked off my shoes and clicked my seatbelt.

"Ain't shit scary bout me ho. I keep a baby Glock in this bag." Eureka pointed to her big wannabe Birkin bag.

"Whatever City Girl. Let's ride. Shit, I got the job."

"Good, it took you long enough. What you went in there to do suck the owner's dick?" She joked as she drove down the street.

I paused for a minute before answering. We didn't keep secrets and she knew how I was hung up on Tom Tom.

"Mmmmmm, yeah I did." I pulled out a stick of gum and begin to chew it. I loved gum and popped it at the most inconvenient times, annoying the hell out of those around me.

"Tell me you're lying!?!" Eureka turned the music down and looked at me over her big sunglasses.

"Nope. It was big and good as fuck too." I was proud to share the tea that I had just committed thot activity.

"Well shit. Ain't nothing wrong with that. That nigga paid like a motherfucker anyway, so go head sis!"

Everyone knew that Avant was paid and his restaurants were doing numbers. He currently had three restaurants with this being his fourth one. He was a fine, single business man so all the bitches were down on him.

"Yeah, I start tomorrow."

"Hot Girl Summer starting off right I see!" E.ureka bounced in the driver seat

We were now back at my house. It was Monday and Eureka didn't have to work because the salon was closed on Monday's unless special appointments were booked. It was not noon yet but it was time to turn up to celebrate the new job. Somewhere in the world, it was happy hour.

Feeling good, I ran upstairs to take a quick shower to wash the sex off me. Today was a really good day. I had gotten a job and some bomb ass dick. When I woke up this morning I was not expecting either.

By the time I came back downstairs wearing some pink biker shorts and a matching crop top, Eureka was at the counter standing like she was bowlegged and pigeon-toed, knowing damn well she wasn't, making frozen margaritas with the music blasting. It was a mood.

"Girl that's what's up you got this job!" She yelled over the music. She had already taken a shot or two the way she sounded.

"Yesss! I'm ready to drink to this."

Wasting no time we had downed a pitcher of margaritas and was on to pitcher number two as we sat at the kitchen table.

My phone started ringing nonstop. It shows unavailable but I know that can only be one person calling me. Reluctantly I answered and followed the prompts.

"You have a collect call from an inmate at City Regional Jail, press one to accept."

It's my man Tom Tom. I pressed the zero to accept. I didn't want to take too long for fear of pissing him off.

"Hey, Tom Tom." I answered dryly.

"Bitch why the fuck you just answering your phone? I've been calling you all fucking morning! What the fuck is the problem?" He sounded like he was in a gym or somewhere with a lot of activity in the background as he yelled at me. I moved my phone back from my face some.

I was so sick of him. We have been together for the last seven years. The best thing to come out of this relationship is my soon to be five-year-old daughter, Tommie and our two year old Taymar. During the seven years together, he spent more time in jail than out of jail. The whole time I've held him down.

When we first met Tom Tom was the man, he was getting money. He was holding shit down. I didn't want for anything but now those days with far and few in between. He called all day long running up my phone bill and he expected me to keep money on the books. The money that he left behind was already dwindling down to the last few hundred dollars. For this bid, he had been locked up this time for eight or nine months. Shit who is counting, his ass stayed locked up these days. I was just so frustrated with him.

"I had an interview today. Money is tight around here so I gotta do something different."

Tom Tom softened up a bit and changed his tune. "Sorry for yelling at you, daddy will be home soon. I will be helping with everything as soon as I get home. You know when I get home baby I'm a marry you right?"

I sucked my teeth because I didn't want to hear this shit. I had heard this all before. He didn't want my ass working and he would say whatever to get on my good side. Eureka looked at me and rolled her eyes. She knew that I could do so much better than him. She had been telling me this for the longest time to get with the program.

"Yeah, I love you too," cooed into the phone trying to keep him going off. Even with the volume down, he would eventually spazz out if he realizes I was having a good time. Instead of him being happy that I was telling him I loved and reciprocating the love he started going off again. It wasn't surprising because Tom Tom really wasn't a nice person, he had an attitude out of this world. Most people assumed that he was in jail for drugs but he was actually sitting down at the city jail because he was arrested for threats and assault. He had attacked someone. His attitude was out of this world.

"What the fuck is that music playing in the back room? It's not even 1 o'clock in the day."

"Nothing. just celebrating my new job with Eureka."

"You know I can't stand that bitch Eureka. You need to find some better friends or something better to do. When I come home all that shit is going to change."

I hoped this conversation would be over sooner than later because I was tired of talking to Tom Tom. He was blowing my buzz.

"Ok baby."

"Magic make sure you send me some money this week."

Then the phone disconnected. I know damn well this nigga didn't just hang up in my face. I just looked at the phone.

"Girl you will not believe the shit this nigga talking about."

"I'm not surprised when it comes to him. I'm not the least bit surprised." Eureka had expressed to me so many times how she felt I could do better and how she didn't care for him, she only tolerated him for the sake of me and the kids.

The way he just tried to handle me the only thing I was mad about was not getting some dick sooner and kicking his ass to the curb. "I'm about to say fuck that relationship. I got moves to make. Let's get this money fuck him!"

"Ayeeeeee! About fucking time! Girl, I'm telling you. Hashtag Hot Girl Summer! You already had a taste of boss today so the sky is the limit bitch. Fuck that miserable ass Tom Tom fucking with him only going bring you down. And fine bitches like us don't sit around and struggle. Boss the fuck up friend!"

Eureka was not ugly but she was not as fine as she thought she was either. My girl thought she was the finest bitch that ever walked the face of the Earth. I mean she was aight, she was right next to me! She jumped out of her chair and begin to shake her big ass. She always rocked long dramatic lashes, long nails and even longer weaves. Being a stylist she loved to play around with her hair styles. Right now she had on her hair in a sleek bob with the sharp ass, Chinese bangs. I wasn't really feeling this style but she rocked it and owned it. Her real hair was long and thick she could have easily wore that but she kept a weave. Her bright lipstick covered her juicy lips. Even though it was loud as fuck it went well with her smooth, butter pecan tan skin tone. Her bodysuit could've been a size bigger. Her clear fanny pack rested on her pudgy midsection she worked hard to hide and she rocked some Balenciaga looking sneakers because we know damn well they were not real.

"It's a new me and a new day."

"Well, bitch I don't care what you do just do good. Make sure the next move is the best move. We going to get this fucking money.It's the summer time and we going have some fun for once. Now give me all the tea about earlier. Your ass not off the hook."

I took another sip of my drink before speaking. "My pussy still over here thanking me. I noticed your ass been really nice lately and I am not the only one who got some shit going on. Let's hear your shit first."

"It's like this, don't be trying to pass no fucking judgment. I can't shake my nigga Boo. I just can't get him out of my system. Then I got the nigga from church on my ass."

"So what are you going to do?"

"I'm in my bag. I'm not turning shit down but my collar. That's not the worst of it all. It's a married nigga I have not given the time of the day. His ass thinks he can buy his way into my life and heart."

"Oh my fucking god. You always got some shit going on girl." I leaned back and fanned myself.

"Yes, he got a whole wife at home. Is it wrong that I don't give a fuck about her though? I need my fucking bills paid and I'mma get it all."

"I mean you are going to do whatever you want regardless of what I tell you."

"Sis I got this under control. Watch how I work. Enough about me back to your mid-day on the low."

The drinks had my girl dancing like she was in the club. Even though I felt nice doing a two-step right now as she killed it. Shit I felt good with the music blasting and the alcohol in my cup.

"He was going crazy. Bitch that nigga was fine dining in a fine dining place!"

"You so stupid."

I looked at my watch, time was getting away from us. My kids would be on the way home soon. "What's your plans for later on today?"

That was my cue for my girl to make moves. She didn't have to go home but she had to get up out of here. We would link later on.

"I got a couple of appointments. One a hair appointment and one a dick appointment."

Couldn't be mad at that at all.

Chapter 2 Eureka

Honey I'm home! Oh, wait. Ain't no damn honey to come home to. I opened the door to my second floor, three-bedroom apartment to get out the damn heat. Messing around with Magic I was tipsy as hell. That damn heat and alcohol was not a good mix. It's so damn hot I swear I passed the devil at the ice cream truck before I walked up the stairs.

Even though I didn't have a man or kids to greet me, the cold air from the AC welcomed me with open arms. I was so thankful I had my own space. For the last four years I'd been working at a salon called Bianca's. I'm not going lie, my ass was living above my means and I could barely afford my booth rent and the high ass rent for this apartment. I can't help my parents raised me to like the finer things in life. I could have easily worked hard but that was not my thing. I wanted everything fast and easy, that's the reason I fuck with niggas with money. If they got money and they are spending it everyone is benefiting.

It would have been easier for me to work on my off days but that was too much like right. I just didn't have time to be working myself to death. My parents had worked their little warehouse jobs forever and a day and they were finally getting ready to retire. I didn't want to be working forever. Nope I sure didn't. I was trying to live my best life and didn't have not one problem making some shit shake for a couple of dollars even if it was my ass!

My big booty jiggled as I walked into the kitchen area and begin to get ready for a client. Some girl had hit me up on IG about an hour ago. I was all about my coins. If she had money I had the time. She was coming to get a sew in. I didn't really take new clients at my house but since she hit me up kind of on some emergency shit and she was willing to pay the fees I told her to come on as soon as that deposit hit my Cash app.

With no time to waste, I quickly prepped the area because once I was done with her I had big shit to handle.

After gathering all my supplies and waiting I decided to throw some chicken breast in the oven and bake a couple of sweet potatoes, making something quick for dinner. No sooner than I slipped off my shoes there was a knock at the door.

I had my apartment laid out like some of those bad ass apartments that went viral on social media. My living room was navy blue and silver. Of course I had the white fluffy pillows and sequined pillows strategically placed on my chairs. I know it was trending to have Marilyn Monroe pictures up but I had large pictures of beautiful chocolate sisters on my wall. I was all about the melanin. I even had photos of myself growing up and pictures of Magic and her kids after all they were my family too. Everything thing in my home was in place and I always received compliments when people saw how I had laid the place out.

The girl standing on the other side of the door complimented me as soon as I swung the door opened. I thanked her and invited her in. I was not about to be cooling off the whole damn neighborhood.

"Come on in." I ushered the girl into the dining area that I designated as my home salon area.

I looked at the her hair when she pulled off her Polo hat, it was all tangled up and uneven. Damn, I had my work cut out. I cringed.

"I know it looks bad Eureka but please fix it! I saw your work on the gram. I told you I'm willing to pay extra if I have to." She begged.

My IG was popping off just my hair styles alone. When I posted my home and pictures of myself looking good as fuck those pictures always did numbers too. I got most if not all of my clientele from social media.

"Oh, you're paying extra for the last minute appointment and all the work I gotta do to bring you back." I laughed. "It's going to take a miracle for me to get you right but sit back. I got you."

I put the cape on the girl and got to work, she was going to need her hair trimmed and deep conditioned before I could even install her bundles.

Normally I charged at least $100 for someone to even think about sitting their ass in my chair at home. The client needs to come with their hair washed, blew out, and trimmed. If they would have come with it braided down that would have made my day too. Just joking. But to look good it was going to cost some money. All my clients knew this when booking with me.

I stopped to take to a few smoke breaks and to talk on the phone. I had to stop to eat dinner before I finally finished with my customer. Shit she ain't mind her ass was fucking that plate up too. If I couldn't do shit else I could do some hair and cook a good meal.

After working miracles on the chick's head by this time I was now exhausted. Spinning her around in the chair to see the results of her middle part sew in, she paid me three, crisp one hundred dollar bills.

"Thank you so much, Eureka."

"Told you I was going get you right." I folded the money and slid it in my bra. I was no joke with my hands. I made good money but not enough money styling hair. I guess it was just the lifestyle I was living.

While doing the girl's hair Boo hit me up. He was the reason I was so nice and generous to my client who just walked out the door, the promise of getting up with him later. Boo was someone I was feeling but the feeling was not mutual. I liked to think "What's understood don't have to be explained" but that nigga was not about to explain anything to me at all.

I ran in the bathroom and took a shower at record speed. I got dressed quickly putting on a bra minus panties, pulling a yellow dress over my head and slipped on some sandals. I drove with a purpose, making my way across town to meet up with Boo. All the lights were green and that was good because I was on go.

In less than fifteen minutes I pulled up beside a black Charger and got in the car with Boo. He wanted to meet by the water. I was on some romantic shit he was just on some shit period.

"Sup, Reka?"

The sound of his voice made my pussy cat quiver. Boo was dark skinned with waves that made me seasick. His beard was big and full. He was making me wet just looking at him. Although he was average looking, his money, big dick, and expensive clothes made him look so much better. It didn't hurt that I had a weakness for dark chocolate men, this one especially. Excited to be in his presence I leaned over to kiss him and he turned to give me his cheek.

"Oh, it's like that Boo?" I frowned my face up, lowkey pissed. I was feeling the fuck out of Boo but he always tried to carry me. The last time we chilled Boo told me that I would look better if I considered getting a tummy tuck and lipo. I swore that was going to be his last time seeing me but here I was again like a hopeless fool in love. I couldn't leave this nigga alone if I wanted to.

"Yeah, it's like that. A couple of weeks you gave me that big ass to kiss when I mentioned getting healthy and fit. I'm shocked you even came out."

I know that Boo liked me but he also knew I had a lot of game. I really believe he was not trying to get caught up so he kept me at a distance. It was only a matter of time before all that changed though. Cut up with a well-defined body, he had mentioned to me about getting healthy and losing weight. He never once came out and said for me to go under anyone's knife, that is what eating right and moderate exercise sounded like to me. I felt like he wanted me to get a whole makeover!

In addition to his own extra- curricular activities, Boo owned his own gym so he was big on fitness. As much as I was feeling Boo, I would do anything for that nigga except take my ass in his gym or have surgery. Take me as I am!

"Aight whatever," I rolled my eyes. "Do you got that money you promised me?" If this is the way he wanted to act I was not about to waste too much of my time out here. I held my hand out.

Boo's voice sounded like it should be on the radio. He already looked like a rapper. In my mind, he was a black god with that dark hard body.

"Yeah but you know what you gotta do for it." The words that flowed from his big, black lips pissed me off but I wanted the money. He waved the bills at me before putting them in the cup holder.

Shit, he ain't said nothing but a word. I didn't mind fucking him for money. He had good dick anyway so I was game. I licked my lips and crawled over closer to him. So much for the date. It wasn't a date if you called dick sucking in a car a date.

With my eyes fixed on his, I lowered her face to his dick and teased the fat mushroom crown, head with my tongue ring. Boo jerked in anticipation when I sucked in the first two inches. Running my hands up and down his legs, I took the full, nine inches of his hard on down with a smile. He let out a deep groan, grabbing my hair, forcing my head up and down his thick rod.

"Oh, suck that shit bitch. Suck it, use a lot of spit!"

The sounds of slurping were very loud as I sucked him off like my life depended on it, in a way it did.

His dick had the thickness of one of those Comcast TV remotes and I attempted to fit all it in my mouth. I let him fill my mouth until I began to gag on the head poking the back of my throat. I could see another three inches left, he couldn't fit in.

His hands wandered down to my big, gigantic ass, using one hand he took hold of my hair firmly, but not to hurt me. He used the grip on my hair to push me down onto his meat, and he filled my throat.

I was such a freak. I loved every moment of this. I paused. "Damn your dick is so big!" He felt between my legs and rubbed my bare pussy. I was not wearing any panties. I was so wet that my juices were seeping down my legs.

I went back down on him getting used to his size, I tried to keep him in my mouth as much as I could while he pushed me down on it.

Then I saw it; he was holding his phone. Boo was recording me sucking his dick. He smiled as he captured the ordeal of me attempting to take his thick dick down my throat.

Instead of being mad, I loved this shit. This only encouraged me more as my lips stretched wide open to take his big pole. That camera was pure motivation.

"Trust me, Reka, nobody else will see this," Boo told me gently stroking my cheek as I went back to sucking his big dick enthusiastically on camera.

Used to being the boss in control, here I was getting recorded sucking dick and he had me gagging and submitting to him. I wanted it regularly with Boo and I could let it all out with him. I wanted to suck him into loving me.

Pushing up his black t-shirt up, I found his wide muscular, chest and felt him up and down as I sucked him for dear life. Boo pulled his big dick out of my wet mouth and recorded as he pressed the thick slab of meat on my face causing me to moan like a bitch in heat.

Standing to attention his dick was in my face, I was staring at its girth as he recorded everything. Seductively for both him and the camera, I licked from the base of his dick all the way up the thick shaft, to his head and back and forth.

"So big." I panted, returning to licking up his shaft once again.

I stared back up at him as he filmed me. I wanted him to see how I handled this motherfucker. He tried to hold back but I was sucking him so good that he had no choice but to moan and let it be known. Throwing up my dress, my naked ass was on camera now. He brought the camera close, showing my ass crack to the screen and began to spread my cheeks. Next, he rubbed my juicy pussy for the camera, all while I continued to worship Boo in my mouth.

Suddenly a phone began to ring; it wasn't Boo's, he was still recording. I was able to reach over to my phone on the seat and view the number I'd saved as Deacon. He was a young nigga from the church who was down on me but I wouldn't give the time of day. I ignored his call as Boo stroked my pussy with two thick fingers, putting me on the verge of a fat ass nut. Deacon could wait. Boo pushed me down on his dick.

I continued to gag and let the phone ring.

"Fuck that nigga. You with me right now, Eureka. Take care of ya nigga." He told me as the phone stopped ringing, and with a moan, I returned to sucking him nodding in agreement as I sucked.

After creaming on his fingers I plopped his erect, hard meat from my mouth. "Strip me." I sat up, trying to gain some kind of control in the situation. Boo knew I was putty in his hands.

He pulled my dress over my head and looked at my thick, fluffy body before he threw it aside leaving me in only my bra. His dick was pulsating, and rock hard in my hands. Looking up, our eyes locked, I stroked as I stared into Boo's eyes. His hands groped and massaged my ass as I looked into his eyes, pumping his rod in my hands. Boo was like steel in my grip, as I saw how aroused he was seeing my chest.

I pushed him back into the driver’s seat. I began to move and grind on his erection pressed against my sweet pussy. Feeling every inch of his impressive, thick tool as I teased him.

Boo didn't need any motivation, he grabbed a hold of my ass. Exposing my big, firm chocolate ass to the camera, I had his big stick standing to attention. I got a grip of his erection and sat on it, sitting down I took him fully inside me and grunted, gasping as he began to push me up and down with his legs.

Our gaze didn't break, our eyes were locked on one another as I rode him like a woman in heat, in love with him. I noticed everything about his face, from the way he clenched his teeth, to the overall effect I was giving him. I had to admit he was the type of man I lusted for. His thick beard tickled me but I kissed him deeply, sliding my warm tongue inside his mouth. This time he didn't turn away from my kisses. I was in control now. Closer to my orgasm I begin to go crazy on the dick, I slammed up and down riding him so good.

I settled into a pace of riding, I began to kiss his chest and up to his broad shoulders, I kissed his neck as I rode him for the gold. My titties still confined to my bra bounced up and down with each stroke.

"Ah, I'm close! I'm going to come baby, I'm going to come, Boo." I threw my head back and screamed panting, my orgasm building up inside as I rode him hard, slamming down onto his rod.

Then I heard him growl, his eyes clenched and his jaw tight beneath his thick beard as I knew he was close to coming inside me. Kissing him hard on his mouth, I felt him inside me and he growled like a bear. He exploded, like a burst pipe inside my juice box.

In unison I exploded with him, bucking my legs I rode him a few more times before collapsing atop of him on his chest for support. Sex with him was always so good. We both panted out of breath, exhausted. Boo leaked inside me, I felt his seed fill my womb, knowing my chances of getting pregnant were slim to none due to my birth control.

I climbed off Boo and reached in my purse for wipes that I carried around just in case for times like this and offered some to Boo. After cleaning myself off, I flipped the visor down and looked at my hair before reaching for her dress sliding it back on.

I wanted to be mad with Boo but after the orgasm he just gave me, I said fuck it.

I wanted to be upset for as long as we've been kicking it, he still treated it like a business arrangement. Breaking the silence I said, "Well I gotta get going Boo."

My dumb ass almost left before he handed me the cash that was in the cup holder. I counted out the money before placing the $300 in my bag.

"When I'm going to see you again, Reka?"

As much as I enjoyed these little fuck sessions I wanted more. I shrugged my shoulders and slammed the door on my way out of the car.

Once home I scrubbed my face, brushed my teeth three times and gargled like that was going to erase the fact that I'd let Boo fuck the shit out of me once again.

After my moment of shame, I pulled my laptop out and began to look up doctors that could do tummy tucks and mommy makeovers. Even though I told Boo I was not going to do anything when it came to my weight, I had been seriously considering going under the knife at 5'6, 250 pounds. Thick in all the right places, my doctor and the medical experts said different. Based on the height and weight chart they told me I was morbidly obese. I felt that shit.

I had struggled with my weight all my life. I had tried all the diets from keto to the Beyonce diet, even trying to exercise but the weight never stayed off. Many considered me a BBW but to me, I was just fat. I mean I wore it well but I was tired of the fupa (my fat upper pussy area) and packing on the extra pounds. Blessed with a big ass, I wanted that snatched waist to match. Maybe if I did this me and Boo could be together.

I made note of a couple of places and decided to call them in the morning. Next, I got in the shower I let the water run over me as I stood there feeling uncertain. I didn't want to just keep fucking I wanted love.

I pulled myself together after my emotional shower and threw on some pajamas and decided to call my mother before heading bed. I was raised by my devout Christian mother and father. I grew up in a Baptist church from Sunday school to bible study, I was in the church from sun up til sun down. My parents lived in the church. The only time I ever got a break was when I went to school. It was at school where I met Magic. We've been friends since the 6th grade. My met in a crowded ass cafeteria and had been best bitches since.

My mother answered on the first ring. "Hey baby," my mother chirped.

"Hey, mom. How are you doing?"

I was now resting in the middle of my queen-sized bed.

"I'm blessed. We missed you in church this weekend baby."

"Mama you know I was busy working all weekend." I lied.

I had missed a few Sundays avoiding Deacon. He was the young, fly nigga who so happened to love God and me. He had been trying to get with me for the longest and I kept brushing him off. Now that I was older I didn't see a need to spend every waking moment in church or donate all that money the way her parents did. My mother wanted me to attend church every Sunday which was not going to happen but I made sure to promise her that I was coming every Sunday. My mother always felt I could use a little more God but I lwas fine with my sinful life but to appease my mother I would go to church at least once a month.

"See if you had a good man you wouldn't have to work so much."

"Don't start mom."

"You know I am not lying. If you had a good, god-fearing man you wouldn't have to work like a slave. Matter fact Jackson asked about you Sunday. You need to give him a chance. Single, no kids, business owner and fine---"

Deacon's government name was Jackson. I called him Deacon because he spent all his time in the church.

"Ok, mama. Anyway, what is Daddy doing?"

"He's in here just watching his shows. You need to think about what I said."

"Ok, mommy I love you. Tell Daddy that I love him too. I'm so tired just finished doing a client's hair at home."

I didn't dare tell my mother that I had gotten my back blown out by a thug nigga.

"Get some rest. I have to work all day tomorrow."

"Ok, ma. Love you."

I closed my eyes and was sleep in no time.

Chapter 3 Magic

"I'll be home soon baby."

When Tom Tom said that I almost dropped the damn phone. What the fuck did he mean he would be home soon? I was not prepared for his shit. How the fuck did he just think he was going to pop out and not give me a date or anything. This nigga thinks he had all the sense in the world.

"Ok. I can't wait." I lied.

I couldn't think of anything better to say. My ass was at loss for words. I thought he still had a few more months left!

"You don't sound happy to be hearin' from your nigga. Say something. You been real moody and having an attitude lately. I'm goin' come home and adjust that attitude real soon. Put this dick on you and daddy going make sure everything is good."

I really couldn't focus on what he was saying. My dumb ass had messed around and fucked my boss Avant and now my man was coming home! All I was worried about was not getting caught up.

"Bae I gotta get ready for work. I told you I got a job at the new restaurant downtown I not too long ago started."

"I heard about that spot... But what you doin working? Didn't I tell you I didn't want you to work? I got us. I don't want my wife working."

He sounded dumb as hell. I was out here with his two kids and no job and he couldn't keep his black ass out of jail. He got a fucking nerve to say he don't want me working. All the damn bills round this bitch needed to be paid. If I didn't do something I was going to be shit out of luck. After telling me he does not want me to work he has the audacity to keep on asking me to send him some money. He hadn't asked for no bread the last few calls so I guess now that he was going to be touching down any day soon he was good on that. Niggas thought they had all the sense in the world.

I looked at my nails. It was time for a much needed trip to the nail salon. I was a bad bitch so I needed to keep up with my looks at all times. I was half listening to him as I mentally counted how much money I had to play around with.

I sighed, "Tom Tom that sound good and all but shit the bills going on. Life is still going on while you biddin'. I gotta go."

Normally his ass was the one hanging up on me but I ended the call before the operator could count down. I had two mouths to feed and was not about to play with his ass. We could sort this shit out if and when he got home. For now, I was going to make me some money.

I already was not used to getting up before noon to punch a clock but I was doing it so my ass wouldn't be homeless, and this nigga was trying to fuck that up. I had been following his ass too long and needed to do me for once.

Work had been so far so good. I had gotten the hang of the waitress and server job quickly. My good looks and bubbly personality had been winning the customers over and I had been receiving good tips. I had not been here a week yet but I felt good earning my own bread and not having to depend on a nigga for shit. I had even managed to avoid seeing Avant. As good as the dick was he was still my boss so I didn't want any confusion. I was happy with doing my job and taking my ass home, after all, I didn't come here to find a nigga or love.

I primarily worked at the busy restaurant, Belle's Kitchen, during lunch hour up until about five. I worked the hours that fit my schedule while my kids are in daycare. Thank god for social services paying for that or my ass would have been fucked. It cost me close to three hundred dollars a week to send my girls to a good daycare center. Lucky for my pockets our oldest would be five by the time school opened in September. Of course, Tom Tom didn't want the kids in daycare. He wanted the kids to go to his great aunt's house, Auntie Reba, who had watched all the kids in his family. I was not sending my kids straight to the damn hood for eight hours a day.

I grew up around that shit and I was not subjecting my kids to it. My kids did not need to be going to the candy lady house to buy loose cigarettes, learning how to shoot dice, at card parties and whatever other shit his aunt Reba had going on at her place. Daycare was right where the hell they needed to be. And I was not going out of my way to go over her place when the daycare was less than a couple of blocks from my house. That nigga was not slick trying to keep tabs on me through his family.

I put the phone call with my nigga behind me and made it through another work. As usual, the restaurant was doing numbers so the time flew by quickly. People could not get enough of that freshly made soul food where they made everyone feel like family. I know I felt good after working here especially since I was bringing in some money of my own.

After counting my tips and gathering my bag it was time for me to head out the door. The food here was so damn good that this place was always packed. Right now the dining area was getting crowded with people who wanted some good soul food that would make you slap your mama and your bald-headed ass sister. I wished I could work later to cash in on the dinner crowd but I didn't have anyone to watch the kids after six so it was time to roll out.

My morning had started off on a bad note talking to my baby daddy but I was good now. I'm sure people could feel the shine from the smile on my face. I was smiling so hard I almost hurt my face.

"Damn some nigga got you smiling I see."

It was none other than Avant's fine self. Once again that nigga was dressed in his finest. His suit fit his body closely and my pussy began to jump immediately. It should be a crime for a nigga to be so fine.

"Hey, you. Ain't nobody got me smiling." I blushed. If he only knew he was causing a whole waterfall between my thighs right now as I stood near the front door. I was trying to make my exit when he met me.

"You sure about that." This nigga was flirting with me openly and I didn't know what to do.

"Yep." There was a silence as we stood there looking at one another. Even in my waitress gear, I was sexy and I knew he could see it. I could see how he was eyeing the cakes.

"So how you like the new job? Is everything going ok for you?"

"It's great I love it and thanks for hiring me I really appreciate it."

"Well Magic, if there is anything that I can do for you please don't hesitate to let me know." I liked the sound of that as the words rolled off his lips.

"I'll have to keep that in mind, Mr. Anderson."

"Avant will do. You weren't calling me Mr. Anderson that day in my office." We shared a look.

Whew, chile! It was getting hot in here. I had to get out of here before this nigga had my ass pressed against the window fucking my brains out or on a table in public! He did something to me.

I laughed. "Well, I gotta get out of here and get my kids. It was nice talking to you."

"I see you in a rush so I'm not going hold you up but we going talk sooner than later."

I didn't want to sound thirsty or say the wrong thing so I just smiled and headed out the door. I had to get to the childcare center in time so I didn't have any late fees. I looked at the clock when I got there I still had a whole twenty minutes before pick up. I scooped up my girls and headed home.

My two daughters were my world. I was going to always make sure they were good at any cost.

I wish someone would have made sure I was good at any cost. My mother had me when she was just 18, right before graduating from high school. She was so embarrassed about being pregnant that my small-framed mom kept me a secret for six months hidden under baggy sweats and oversized clothing until my grandmother suddenly noticed how her stomach was getting bigger and asked if she was pregnant.

Up until this time, everyone just assumed my mother was a stud or some shit. Nobody had no idea she had been getting dicked down on a regular basis. Her and my father had been sneaking around fucking and nobody had suspected a thing because she hung around the guys like she was one of the guys. The first time they had sex it was of a bet. All his niggas had been trying to push up on her saying they bet she had some good pussy since she was not out here fucking everything moving. While they were all talk, my father was about that action and put the moves on my mother. His boys didn't have a clue. If them niggas only knew.

Once my father got a taste of that sweet, virgin pussy he was hooked. They were fucking every chance they got. It was crazy as hell. Behind clothes doors, he was fucking the lining out of her platinum, top-notch pussy and she loved it.

My mother didn't even let my father know she was pregnant with me. She thought he was going to flip out about having me since they were supposed to be best friends. As if things couldn't be worse, he denied ever fucking with my mother because of his stuck up girlfriend. All that came to a wrap as soon as my no-nonsense grandma got whiff of the pregnancy. She pulled up on my father and his family and who wasn't too thrilled or elated to have another mouth to feed but they softened up to the idea of me when I was born.

Shortly after I was born, my grandmother took over and raised me. Motherhood was not something she ever wanted so my mom fled with a new man who filled her purse and her pussy, leaving me behind in the income-based apartments called the Gardens. Gone were the days of her dressing like a nigga. My mother had come into womanhood and all the hood niggas wanted her so she took the opportunity to run off with a boss, giving the hood her ass to kiss.

I later found out the only reason my mother was dressing as one of the boys was to hide her body from her older cousin Man Man, who had been trying to fuck on her. His perverted ass was now in jail with his bitch ass. Man Man had moved in with some older woman with teenage daughters that he started fucking. Bad enough the damn woman had let him move in and he spent all her money but this low life was balling up her daughters and having a relationship with one of them.

Thanks to his piece of shit ass my mother hid behind her good looks. I was not sorry to hear about his pedophile ass going to jail. The only regret and sadness I had were that my mother had got with a savage in her attempts to make boss moves and left me behind. The only thing she was worried about was her money but hey it was typical hood life.

Everyone was broke but hood rich, in other words exhibiting flamboyant spending habits, while doing nothing to improve one's living conditions. My grandmother raised me and my cousins in her three-bedroom apartment that was a revolving door for any family members who needed a pallet or couch to crash on. She didn't work she collected checks, sold dinners and whatever else she needed to do to get money. That's where I lived with my family until I was 9 when public housing decided they were going to shut them down and renovate them. That was just an excuse for the city to make for gentrification and move everyone closer out of the heart of the city.

In fact, we moved to a worse public housing project called Crimson Heights. It was there that I became closer to my father's side of the family because this is where he was from. I stayed there until I was 18, which is when I left to do my own thing with a nigga who was my everything, Tom Tom. I wish I could say since then, I've only been back a few times and none in the last decade but my ass went out there every chance I got to stunt on bitches and flex on niggas.

***

"When you say my name say that shit twice. Tom is my name and a nigga is nice."

We've been rocking strong now since I was almost a woman. Light skin with pretty eyes and a body marked up with ink from his face to his feet, he stole my heart without ever saying a word to me. All the girls in my hood wanted a chance to get under that strong body and be called his girl.

It's crazy how he didn't even know I existed or barely spoke two words to each other, like ever. I would push my ass out and perk my titties up and pretend to be bowlegged as I walked to the basketball court or to the store with my girl Eureka just to get a chance to see him. I wanted him so bad that I had to have him. Any niggas with eyes could see I was that bitch, but he didn't pay my ass any mind.

After enough chasing him I said fuck it and decided when the right time came, he would be mine. Of course, I had to play hard to get when that time came. That nigga couldn't just think I was some easy pussy.

Fat Meme was having a cookout. She was this big girl who thought because she was loud with a bunch of dope dealing brothers she was the shit. I mean she was cool or whatever but she wasn't shit. Me and Eureka were going so we could be the center of attention and get some free food and drinks. I had gotten Eureka to braid my hair and we had gotten outfits from the mall compliments of the five-finger discount just to make sure we were on at the party. I had to make sure I was hitting at all times. These bitches out here loved to hate on us.

"Them bitches going hate on us tonight!" I yelled as I winded my body in the mirror. Best had laid my hair and it was time to show out.

"Bitch them down on their luck hoes always hating on us!" Eureka high fived me.

Satisfied with our appearance we headed to the cookout. Cars were lined up down the street for two blocks. The whole city came out so I hoped that it would not be any shit tonight. In the event of any disagreement, niggas didn't just square up and fight they would want to air out the whole damn party. I looked way too good to be running and dodging bullets and shit tonight so I said a silent prayer when we hit the yard.

The party was so close to our hood that it was no point in driving only to have to find a parking spot a mile away. I didn't have a car yet. Eureka had a car that her parents had gotten her last year when she turned sixteen. It was almost brand new, with rims on it. When I say we rode that wheels off that bitch. Today instead of pushing her whip we were out here throwing shade and ass when we walked up in this bitch.

Looking around the party was lit. It was so much food and drinks. There were hella niggas in here. Paid ones, broke ones, fine ones, and even ugly ones. The only nigga that mattered to me was the one who I was leaving with and that was with Tom Tom.

The moment I was waiting for had finally happened. We were finally up close and personal.

"It's good to finally kick it with you. I'm Magic."

"I already know who you are. Trust me I've seen you in the hood. Lucky for you I haven't heard your names ran by none these niggas out here."

"Naw for real I be cooling. I'm about my money and that's it. I don't have time for these niggas. I am not trying to be nobody's baby mama or none of that shit."

"Smart girl. I would never want you to be just a baby mama. I would make you my everything."

I smiled. Damn this nigga was a boss.

Even though we had made that introduction I still had to play hard. I walked off because I knew he would want me.

It was that cliché thing where Tom Tom asked for my number and I said no. He asked again and I said no. He asked me again and again and I said no, no, no.

It wasn't until near the end night that I saw him again. He saw me like glued to my phone and I remember he just came up to me, grabbed my phone, and took it away from me. And then he took his own phone out of his pocket and gave both of our phones to his friend and he asked me to go on a walk with him. Sometimes, I wonder what would have happened if I hadn't gone on that walk. Within five minutes, he won me over. I mean I didn't make it obvious to him at all that he won me over, he had no idea, but I swear he won me over.

From day one I had been fucking with a savage. He got into a fight that night actually. It's weird to think back to it now—how I didn't turn away at the first sign of trouble. Some guy at the party said something dumb to his friend, and they got into a fight and I think he hit him with a bat. I mean I knew that this other guy ended up leaving the party bloody because of what my man did to him. But I didn't turn away.

Before I decided to get with him this nigga was living his wild lifestyle. Before he was with me he was selling drugs and hustling. He always dealt like petty drugs all throughout high school. But it would be like selling weed or "E" or something like that. And that was fine.

It was all fine until one day, it wasn't just to other kids at school, and it definitely wasn't just weed. He graduated from high school to the streets. He went from selling weed to cocaine. When that wasn't enough, he begins pushing crack to fiends and strung out mothers. It was crazy who copped from him. He had women offering themselves to him to chase that glass dick. Even men who got up and went to work all week just to blow that whole paycheck in a couple of hours on Friday was running him down for a hit. It didn't matter who wanted to get high as long as they had money he was going to serve them. Tom Tom was moving up in the rankings in the drug game and I was right there with him as his lady.

Recently his drug of choice was dog food. Just as fast as crack hit the streets people were now riding that train. As long as people had money Tom Tom was going to give people what they wanted. He lived to sell drugs, that was like his high.

I should have walked away a thousand times but I stayed because I loved my man. I guess just being mixed up in that crowd, not even just dating a drug dealer, but just being around that lifestyle, things happen. My tires have been slashed, my windows have been broken, stuff like that. I've had a few fights with bitches who couldn't walk a mile in my shoes. I'm sure I've heard more gunshots than most people do in a lifetime.

I remember this one moment where I had to kind of take a step back and was just like whoa, "What is happening?"

We were at a party and one thing led to another and a nigga there got stabbed. I saw a knife pierced into his body—just sticking out of him. Blood everywhere and people were just trying to get out of the way. I moved my feet so fast trying to get away I almost tripped over a couple of bitches trying to get to my man. My one and only thought was is he good? And that wasn't even the weirdest part. The weird part was after I found out Tom Tom was good, we sat down and I ordered Waffle House. I just went and ordered a steak, eggs and a waffle with jelly on the side.

Like what?! What was I doing with my life?

I realized how desensitized I had gotten to all this craziness. I mean I grew up in the hood but I was never this involved in shit. I was really out here riding for Tom Tom. I started thinking and it really freaked me out. This was before the kids came along. Now I felt like I was stuck with his ass.

Chapter 4 Avant

Looking around at my surroundings, I was thankful and very blessed. I grew up in a fucked up place that I would never want to live in again. The projects destroy the future of most people but it made me very thankful for small things.

I grew up were people promoted ignorant ass values and shit, have kids early, those kids get indoctrinated with the same ignorant values, and the cycle repeats itself for generations. But I made it out. Actually, "survived" is more accurate because there are many things that can imprison a nigga in the hood forever. I could have gotten a girl pregnant as a teen, I had my share of pussy. Chicks threw themselves at fine niggas like me on the daily. It would have been nothing for a chick to try to pin a baby on me and make a come up out of their mama's house.

I didn't want any part of that shit. Even though we lived in the hood my father was in my life and he made sure me and my sister didn't want for shit. When I was like sixteen I was out here with a pack myself so my mother didn't have to struggle. It was like I had two lives. One with my mother and one with my father.

Living in the fast lane I could have easily been arrested or killed. It wasn't easy, but I avoided all these things. In a sense, all my life a nigga had to fight.

I learned things from that environment which give me a significant advantage outside of the hood. And the things I learned are very different from book learning. This is the type of education you can only experience, survive, and then say to yourself, "Never again." Street smarts.

My home situation was slightly better than average when compared to the typical shit that went on in my hood. My mom didn't always work, but she took temp work when she could and I never went hungry. I didn't live with my dad but he was always in the picture. My mom didn't bring any men around after her one and only boyfriend beat me and my sister badly.

Safe to say my father beat the fuck out of that nigga. I loved my father to death. He was not a street nigga but a regular 9-5 nigga. He got up and went to work everyday and made shit happen for us but him and my mother couldn't work on their relationship. I think it was because he was a very handsome man and my mother was a jealous woman. Instead of them arguing all the time they just parted ways.

Me and my sister looked forward to the weekends when our father would come get us. He lived in the county away from all the drama of the city. It was there where me and my sister would learn how to cook and spend time with my great grandmother who was my restaurant's namesake.

My father was a rather stand up guy and he always told me "Son keep your head in the books and stay out of the streets." I felt that shit. I always wanted to make him proud.

Even though I did the right thing I was still a nigga from the hood. My father would have all these talks with me and push me towards greatness when I was with him but I had to go back home to my mom in the hood so I was learning to live life on both sides. Because of my father, I went to college. He was the reason I was able to get my business up and running.

When he died he left me and my sister a $50,000.00 insurance policy. That is the money I used to boss the fuck up with. I was just trying to live my life and stay out of shit.

I lived in a recently built four-bedroom house. It would definitely be nice to have someone to share this big house with but instead, I lived alone. I've been considering lately settling down with a good woman if I could find one. My last relationship of three years with my baby mama Leshaniqua ended because she didn't have the same vision as me.

Twenty-eight years old and single, I own three soul restaurants and just opened a fourth location. I wanted to run a successful empire and her ass wanted to r un the streets. The only good thing that came out of the relationship was my daughter. It was no doubt in my mind that my baby mama had tried to trap me.

Refusing to get stressed out thinking about her I cooked a small dinner for myself of steak and roasted potatoes. I poured me a drink of Hennessey. I did have one good thought on my mind. That sexy ass Magic.

I wasn't looking forward to doing a last minute interview this is what I paid my staff to do. I knew the moment I laid eyes on Magic shit was going to be crazy. She came in fidgety and her resume was all balled up. To make matters worse she spilled water all over the damn thing. Her good looks saved her. Lucky for her I wanted pretty smiling faces in my restaurant to greet and serve the customers.

I just hope that it didn't get out so the rest of my staff what had happened. I tried to be discreet but there was no being the discreet the way she was carrying on in the office. I had to put my hand over her mouth quiet her. I was still shocked by what we had done. I could've had any woman I wanted and yet I fucked the help.

Chapter 5 Eureka

The only god I was going to be getting closer to tonight was my nigga Boo. Every time I talked to my mother she was on the same shit. It didn't matter if it was the next day or the next week but my mother always presses me to come to bible study. She wanted me to come tonight but that was a negative. If it was up to her I would have been present at any and every church function! I was taking a rain check tonight because I was going to do my god daughters' hair for Magic then get up with my man. In that order.

I had been on my feet all day in the salon working my fingers to the bone. I was really getting tired of slaying all these heads in here while the owner Bianca walked around like her shit didn't stink. If this bitch kept this shit up, I was going be out of this joint sooner than later. I was already paying this high ass both rent that I could barely afford but to be loaded with her clients that I was not being paid for was larceny. Petty fucking larceny!

The only reason I stuck around was that her shop was booming and I knew I could get a lot of clients and make money fast but I didn't like anyone taking my kindness for weakness.

I swear bitches think they can do whatever they want when you are not a licensed cosmetologist. I was going take my state boards and show this heifer a thing or too real soon. That is what pushed my ass to grind so hard daily but the slick shit Bianca was doing made it really hard to keep my peace. I put my airpods in my ear and blocked those whores out for the most part.

Once my last client was done I hauled ass out the shop, Bianca and her messy ass sister Jaz could kiss my ass. One day I was going walk out this bitch and never come the fuck back. Even though it paid the bills I felt like I was hustling backward there.

It didn't take me long to do my little boo's hair. I cornrowed their hair and put beads on it. Magic had washed it before I got here to speed shit up.

"You need to let me do something to your hair Magic." I looked over at my best bitch. She had that big ass fluffy poof on her head. All she did was put that shit in a puff or a high bun.

"I don't got no money for your high ass prices."

"Bitch you never pay me, so cut it out. Shit, I'm hungry you ain't cook shit. Let's go get something to eat. Fuck it let's get some drinks too."

"All you want to do is drink bitch. I don't have a baby sitter. I can't do shit tonight."

"What's wrong with Auntie Reba? She always wants them. Your bougie ass just don't take them over there. Shit, a couple of hours wouldn't hurt shit."

"You know I don't like going over there. I don't want Tom Tom people all in my damn business."

"You make me sick. I guess I'll go out on my own then. I was treating and everything and you wanna act like that."

"If you paying let me make that call now. You never volunteer to pay for shit."

Magic called Auntie Reba and got the kids ready. While she was handling the kids I was going home to get myself together. It was a good thing we only stayed right around the street from one another.

"I'm going to get dressed. Come over my crib and scoop me when you're done. Since I'm paying the least you can do is drive."

Magic drove a late model black Lexus. Tom Tom kept her in a nice car. I mean my shit was a late model but it damn sure wasn't any luxury vehicle or whatever so we were taking her car tonight.

When I got home I got dressed. I slicked the edges down on my frontal ponytail. That was my style for the next week or two. I was undecided about this style because the lace was cutting off my damn forehead and cutting it close to my eyebrows. People told me that it looked good but I don't know. Them hoes was sharing the fuck out of my frontal ponytail hair styles on social media. Maybe they really fucked with the hair style or were just fucking with me. Bitches lie to you in a heartbeat.

I piled gel on the back of my hair that didn't match the smooth, silky texture of the frontal, that shit needed to be relaxed for real. A bitch won't going tell me to my face I was not fine as fuck. I wished a bitch would!

I put on a waist trainer underneath my bodysuit so I wouldn't be out this bitch looking like a wrestler from the 80s or 90s. I did any and everything to hid my little gut except follow a good diet and exercise, from diet pills, to waist trainers, to plastic wrap and Vicks vapor rub on my belly. I had to work with what I had shit. I put on some cute platform sandals to set the fit out. Fendi kind of mood! You already know it was not real, it was some online boutique shit, but I looked really good. Bitches in the hood loved to give the impression they could afford high end designer. Yep, its me. I am bitches!

My lashes were long and dramatic as me and my face was beat. I couldn't wait to step out even if nothing but dinner and drinks with my best bitch. Let me check some shit off right quick. My big look alike Birkin bag had good money in it, the ass was fat in the suit, and hair was laid. I was ready to be out heretonight!

Magic was outside laying on the damn horn. She had taken all day and now wanted to rush me. I locked up and headed down to the car. When I got in my bitch was looking good in her lime green, long sleeve shirt and matching biker shorts. She had on clear pointed, pumps showing off the vanilla, white toe nail polish. My bitch must have got that fit from Fashion Nova or one of these bitches that be selling clothes out the crib instead of a boutique. I had just seen a girl from around the way selling the whole damn fit on IG.

"Ayeeee!!!! I see you bitch. We look good as fuck tonight. I love my nieces but let's get them to Auntie!" The girls were in the backseat chilling in their car seats playing on their tablets.

I put on my seatbelt and was ready to ride. When we pulled up to Auntie Reba's hood it was a regular ass day in the hood. When we first turned the corner, people were standing on in front of the brick wall that was divided the backyard from the street on the main court. It was a shit of niggas standing around. They were looking but they knew better. Everyone knows that Magic is Tom Tom's bitch. They went back to mean mugging and their regular scheduled bullshit.

Girls were walking up and down the sidewalk. That was us back in the day, hot as a bitch wanting to catch a hood nigga's eyes. The basketball court was jumping as usual with cars lined up and down the street as niggas balled hard as a bitch. Kids were at the playground and the community center running around with icees in styrofoam cups. Then there were the bad ass little boys on scooters and hoverboards who taunted some of the other kids. All the nosey ladies who sat on their front steps sat out drinking their cheap ass beer and chained smoked catching the gossip fake waved. Some people had grills out cooking and I know that chick who sold dinners was making her bread today the way everyone was out. This was just a day in the life in the hood. Hate it or love it this is where we came from.

I even spotted some of the old, hating ass bitches in our age range who had fucked around and gotten pregnant without a title to a nigga or a car lingering around outside mad with the world. It was nobody's fault but their own that they had mismanaged the fuck out of their box. That hot and ready pussy had gotten them nowhere but the daman hood with a bunch of kids repeating the cycle.

Of course, we passed a couple of bitches out with bonnets and pajama pants on. There were even a few bitches outside sitting on milk crates eating crab legs talking loud as hell. Riding out here you could expect to see just about anything. We just cruised through until we reached the back where Auntie Reba lived.

As usual, her house was jumping like a Friday on the first of the month. People were in and out of the house. She stood at the door tall as the door. She had the same hazel eyes as her nephew Tom Tom.

Come to think of it his whole damn family had those funny ass eyes, even my god daughters.

"It's jumping like a bitch out here today." I got excited. Hell I might pull up on one these niggas and get lucky real quick.

"Hell yeah. We going to make this real quick."

Well that was the end of that idea. I still hung around here from time to time but Magic hated it. I loved everything about my hood, this shit was my playground when it came to these niggas. For real I would have been cool just hanging out here pissing these bitches off but Magic was not having it. I couldn't blame her though because these thirsty bitches out here were mad disrespectful and loved to keep her man's name on their mouth.

I helped her grab the kids out the back before she changed her mind about going out. I knew how Magic ass could be. If she was going out we were getting to it.

"What up Auntie Reba."

"Don't come with that fake shit Eureka. You or this one think yall too good to come to see an old lady. Bring my babies in the house now." She smirked at us both.

Even though she lived in the hood her place was nice as hell. Auntie Reba was hood rich. That family knew how to get some damn money. The kids looked to be happy to be with their family as they went over to their cousins. It was no lie she always watched her family members children.

Her house was lit right now. She had boxes of Churches chicken and Dominos Pizza on the counter along with a cooler filled with drinks near the table. Her pantry door was open and that motherfucker was stacked with food. The kids damn sure were not going to go hungry over here tonight.

Magic spoke. "Well, they are all yours for the night."

Auntie Reba opened her Pepsi that was on the cocktail table before taking a swig. "I told you to bring them damn kids over here. Stop being hardheaded Magic. Shit, I know shit a little tight with Tom in the bing. I love my nieces though."

"Thanks again. I appreciate you watching them on short notice."

We were at that hard metal screen door ready to cross the threshold. The girls didn't even pay our ass no mind as we were leaving.

"It's no problem Magic. I swear it ain't. You picking Tom up Friday when he gets out? When you pick the kids up we need to talk about the party."

It was starting to get dark outside now. I was ready to go out and get some alcohol in my system. Damn was she going talk us all the way to the car. Each step we took she followed but that right there stopped Magic in her tracks. I could tell by the look on my bitch face she didn't have a clue about that release date or the party.

"Yeah."

She hit the unlock button and we got in the car. She pulled off and begin going off.

"That nigga gets out in a couple of days and ain't said shit. Got me thinking he gets out in a few weeks or some shit. What kind of shit he on?"

"That's foul as fuck. Don't stress that shit. We going out and have a good time tonight. Put his ass out your mind til tomorrow morning. Positive vibes only!"

"Yeah, I'm done with that shit. He can take his ass to Auntie house for all I care. I'm ready to do me! Where are we going anyway?"

"I was thinking about your job. You know they have shit going on and it's always a nice crowd. I have slid through a couple of times."

Magic side eyed me. "I don't wanna go to my damn job. I am already there five days a week."

"Girl I want a chitlin plate with some of that macaroni and collards, so yeah we are going there. And shit they got strong drinks."

Magic sucked her teeth and shit. I know how she could be petty, so I was shocked when she pulled up to Belle's Kitchen. There was even someone at the front like this was a real live club behind the rope and everything letting people in. She looked over at me.

"Eureka, honey chile, I want you on your best---"

I laughed. "My best bullshit! I'm going to get me some food and drinks and have a good time as you need to be doing. Your bossy ass husband will be home soon and all your fun will be cut out."

"Girl bye! Let's go show out."

We stepped out the car throwing our ass in a circle. My pussy print was sitting just right in my body suit and the waist trainer put my fupa in check so a bitch couldn't tell me shit. I was here fucking up enough plates on a daily, so we didn't have to wait in line and the fact that Magic was a prized employee here we went straight inside.

We headed to the tables closer to the bar and took a seat. I was so glad that my girl had got her ass out of the house. The dj was playing music and it was a full house of people that appeared over twenty-one in the building. The waitress took our order and I made sure to order my girl a strong stiff ass drink.

"You know what bring us back two shots each and let me get two of those drinks." I pointed to the jungle juice in a big vase looking container on the menu. That would be a good start for us. Tonight we were going to get real tipsy.

In no time the drinks were flowing and we were having a good time. When my server brought my plate out I could have kissed her. The cornbread was light and fluffy looking like it had been made in heaven's kitchen, my macaroni was bubbly and cheesy, the greens were also dead ready. Just as I poured hot sauce over the delicate platter of chitlins and savored my first bite, while Magic scrunched up her face in disgust, I noticed Deacon by the bar looking at me.

What the fuck was he doing here?

6'4, size 12 shoes, he reminded me of that fine ass Dave East. I was not expecting to see him here. I hoped and prayed he kept his religious, spiritual ass at that bar. I knew that was not the case when he came striding his tall sexy self in this direction with a mischievous smile.

"Eureka what the hell you doing? You died for them funky ass chitlins now you acting like you lost your appetite all of a sudden?" She turned around and saw Deacon walking this way.

"Bitch! I was not expecting to run into him."

"Fuck all that! Who is he? You ain't tell me about him. All I ever hear about is that black ass Boo. I know this nigga ain't nobody's husband so who is he?"

She waited for my explanation. I couldn't do shit because I was tongue tied trying to get my lies straight. By then it didn't matter anyway because he was standing right at our table smiling at me. He was kind of tall so he leaned over towards me.

"Hello, ladies. Sorry, we missed you at bible study tonight Eureka. Your mother said you were going to try to make it."

“Yeah, I had to do my nieces’ hair so I couldn’t make it.” That part wasn’t a lie.

Magic sat there watching us like we were a damn movie. I kicked her under the table. Good thing the table had a tablecloth so nobody could see it. She gave me an evil eye as she glared at me.

“Magic this is Jackson, from my church. Jackson this is my best friend Magic.” I wouldn’t dare call that nigga Deacon to his face. He was standing right here, right now looking too good to be true. He had on all white from head to toe, looking like a tall glass of milk. Deacon wore the white tee, white jeans with a designer belt and white all-over spiked, red bottom sneakers very well. From looking at him he didn’t look like a nigga that lived in the church and openly talked about Christ. I mean he was heavenly though.

I couldn’t take my eyes off his lips as he spoke. I loved a nigga with a fresh haircut, even his facial hair was perfectly trimmed. His cologne had begun to invade my nose as he stood this close to me. I could smell Creed a mile away and it always made me hot.

“Nice to meet you Magic. Eureka use my number sometimes, please. It would be nice to fellowship with you more.”

The waitress interrupted this little impromptu meeting when she came over to bring him his carryout bag. Had she not come over his ass probably would still be running his mouth about church.

Magic couldn't wait for him to walk off. "Bitch you been holding out! That nigga trying to lay hands on you and have you speaking in tongue. Don't lie and tell me you not feeling him."

Of course, I had to downplay it as I shrugged my shoulders. "I mean he aight. You know I got a man. Boo is my nigga."

"If you don't stop playing."

I put my food in a to-go box and continued conversing with my best bitch.

"I don't want no nigga all in the church. I want me a thug nigga that's going beat the pussy up and pay a few bills. Deacon going wanna take shit slow and make everything about church. He looks like the wait until marriage type. Some I'm celibate bs. I'm good."

"Don't miss your blessing fucking around."

"Never that. Boo coming over later on tonight."

"Don't wanna hear about it." Magic playfully stuck her fingers in her ears.

Payback was a mother. I smiled at my best friend. Now it was time to tease her. "How are you going act when a fine, paid nigga pulls up on you? Do you wanna hear that? What you going do Magic?"

It was Magic's turn to be shocked as Avant stepped to her. That's what her ass got for trying to get all in my business. She was talking about me when that nigga had her ass blushing and smiling. That little romp in the office must have been something tough the way he had her cheesing.

Our night out was just what the hell we needed. I was glad my girl had got out of the house. She had spent way too much time being loyal to Tom Tom. It was time her ass was deciding to live. I know I was damn sure going to live my best life. My girl didn't have to say it but I know she was going back for seconds the way she looked at that nigga.

Magic had dropped my ass off at home and I was good on that because I was going to chill until my man came over. Boo was bringing that big, black snake over. That was going be the icing on the cake tonight. I mean for real he could ice me out and glaze me up. I needed my weekly fix of him and his money. I lay in bed in my lingerie waiting on him to come. I wanted him to walk straight in and fuck the shit out of me. I had given Boo a key to my apartment so he could let himself in at times like this.

An hour had passed and I was still watching hair videos on YouTube waiting patiently for this nigga. I was planning on putting this tipsy cat on him and he was not here yet. After about two hours I started to blow up his phone. I could tell he was ignoring me and pushing end on my calls. After about five or six calls he must have powered the phone off.

Fuck Boo with his black ass!

By now I was screaming on his voice mail, “Man fuck you Boo! You have no concept of quality time. This shit is dead. Your idea of an outing includes running the streets and making moves like a fake boss does; I am not Bonnie nor are you, Clyde! Then you stand me the fuck up! I hate your ass.”

Count your days Boo. We were fucking done! His ass was not about to keep fucking me over.

Chapter 6 Avant

The room is dark but there are stars illuminating the ceiling shining on her black body as I watch a bad ass dancer gyrate her sexy body on the pole.. It's a sight to behold. I'm on cloud nine watching Magic work the pole. She really is black girl magic. Her body is moving all seductive as she is riding the beat of the song.

After she dropped her friend off, she came back over here and we've been chilling. Normally people get to know one another then fuck but we had fucked each other senseless and now we're getting to know one another. She was more than just a fuck. Magic had many layers to here I was determined to reach them all.

She made me want her in the worst way as I sat back in the chair and threw bills at her ass as she danced for me. One thing I liked about her was that she was cool and carefree. We were past all that nervous shit from when we met at the interview now. Magic was coming out of her shell and I loved it.

"You like what you see Avant?" She crawled over to me.

"Hell yeah. You working the fuck out the pole. Now come work this one." I looked at my manhood that was rising. I wanted her to work my pole but I had patience. The night was still young.

After working her fine body on me teasing me to the point of me almost coming in my pants she walked away showing me all of her curves. She jumped back to her dancing, further hypnotizing me with her eyes never leaving mine. When the song went off she collected her money. It was close to a thousand dollars.

At this moment I was glad I had the pole installed in my basement. The room was decorated like a small bar with flat TVs on the wall, a pool table in the center and a bar against the right side of the room. The pole was in the back in the corner on a stage. Other than the pole my favorite thing in this room was the large fish aquarium I had in the room filled with colorful fish.

I had taken her on a tour of my house and she immediately ran to the stage. Normally I didn't bring females over my house but she just gave off a good vibe, so I just wanted her to be comfortable. Of course, I had Alexa and the surround sound in the room so when Magic kicked off her heels and started gyrating to the music I sat my ass down and loosened my tie as she put on a hell of a performance. I had no issue with throwing the two stacks of money at her fine ass.

Magic put her money on the bar then sat down on my lap.

"That was fun Avant."

"Who you telling," that was more of a statement than a question. "I was not expecting you to get up there and do that."

"Me neither. I have never done no shit like that in my life."

I kissed her on the lips. She must have been waiting on that moment the way she kissed me back. I palmed her ass and rubbed all over her soft body. I wanted to fuck the shit out of her right now.

"Let's go upstairs."

"Lead the way." She said.

We made our way to my living room.

"I love your house Avant. Why a man like you got all this space?"

"I'll be here all night explaining my shit to you."

"I don't have no curfew. I've got the time."

I was just about to fuck her silly and now she wanted to talk. I made myself comfortable beside her on the chair. I gave her the run down on how I was single with a daughter and a baby mother from hell. *Why the hell couldn't some females let it go when the shit was over?*

"So what's your story Magic? Why some nigga ain't tied you down?"

"I got two kids. I just not too long ago ended a relationship. I'm just doing me right now."

"I feel you. All I want to do is get this money and take care of my daughter."

I showed her a picture of my daughter on my phone. She was my pride and joy. She in return pulled out her phone and showed me pictures of her girls. They were beautiful brown babies like their mother.

"Your baby mama gotta be dumb to let a fine nigga like you go. You seem to have all your shit together. I'm trying to get my shit together now."

"Believe it or not that's one of the reasons me and my baby mama Leshaniqua didn't work out. She doesn't want to do shit but bitch and complain, accuse me of cheating and make my life hell."

"With a name like Leshaniqua, I am not surprised about anything she does or says. That should have been a red flag that bitch was going to make your life hard and not your dick."

If I could take it back I would have skipped past my baby mother the day I met her.

Bm had been blowing up my phone.

"We need to talk right now Avant."

Uh oh. I didn't know what the hell she could possibly want but I dropped what I was doing and went to her place. Leshaniqua dropped a bombshell on me.

She was pregnant. Then, after the most stressful half hour of my life of her crying crocodile tears and snot on her face, she told me she wasn't actually pregnant and just wanted to see what I would do if she was.

"I'm not pregnant Avant. I just wanted to know how you act if I was." She was the color of peanut butter with long dark hair she kept in an ice cream cone bun laid with baby hairs. She had a nice little body for someone who didn't work out and ate wings and subs from the corner store all day.

She was a hood rat chick that didn't give a shit about anything but me. Leshaniqua never had a problem dropping to her knees and sucking the soul out of my dick. In return, I blessed her with all my inches. That was about the only thing in check. Even though she was a hot girl, she was a rowdy female that just had way too much fire. Besides the good pussy and fire head, she was loyal to me. That's what made me lock her down.

I had been dealing with her mood swings and feisty attitude but this shit here was stupid.

"Why the fuck would you play about some shit like that. Even though the time is not right because I am building up my restaurants you know how much I want a baby."

I had recently opened a second restaurant. Business was booming. I had named the establishment after my great grandmother and I had used some of her recipes and employed some of my family in the kitchen to let her good cooking live on. I was busting my ass to stay on the right side of the law. I was never going back to that street shit. Life was looking up.

I had plans to build a new house, the money was flowing in. Everything was good except for this lukewarm relationship. Leshaniqua was blowing me because the more I wanted it was the less she wanted. Now her ass was sitting up here faking pregnant. I could not deal with this stupid shit.

I noped out of that relationship immediately, by which I mean I continued seeing her for another month because sticking your dick in crazy is still fun. Now she really was pregnant.

I had knocked her ass up so I felt stuck with her. I was not about to leave my baby with a trap queen mama so I tried my hardest to make things work. But as usual, she pulled another stunt.

Now she was pressing me for a ring. It was still early in the pregnancy. Tonight was a regular ass date night. I was trying hard to make this shit work and keep some kind of spark although she was making it hard. Leshaniqua constantly accused me of sticking my dick in other women. She stalked my social media page. Ratchet as she was, she held down a job as a supervisor working in a call center but being two months pregnant warranted maternity leave in her eyes.

I was stuck dealing with a crazy emotional ass female. I was willing to stick it out for my baby to have a two-parent household. At this point I was claiming it to be a girl, I just wanted my baby girl to have a normal family. I probably would have married my bm if she was not bat shit crazy.

My ex somehow thought that taking her to a fancy dinner meant that I was going to propose to her. All I was trying to do was have a good meal and take her out.

"I know why you brought me here Avant and I want to say yes baby I will marry you. Yes, baby. I am willing to spend the rest of my life with you as Leshaniqua Anderson."

She looked at me with tears in her eyes.

"What the hell are you talking about girl?" I was clearly confused.

"Didn't you bring me here to propose to me?" She looked around.

From the crisp white tablecloths to the candles and rose centerpieces, with smooth jazz providing background music, and the subtle lighting leaning toward dim for a romantic ambiance she was way out of her element. Fine dining, just as the name suggests, offers patrons the very best in food, service, and atmosphere and right now I was just trying to give her a great experience and this fool was talking about a fucking wedding proposal.

Many people choose fine dining restaurants for special occasions but I just wanted to have dinner somewhere decent. If she was going to be fucking with me she was going to have to get used to the best things in life.

Leshaniqua looked around as patrons were escorted to their table, and waiters held the chairs for women. I guess she was expecting me to slide a ring on her finger. I simply made reservations to check out the place. I had been hearing nothing but great things and I wanted inspiration in case I ever decided to do a fine dining place instead of the casual, soul food places I owned.

"No, baby I am not proposing to you. This is simply dinner."

She looked like she was about to turn up in the restaurant. If she did I would not have been the least bit surprised. We ended dinner early and left.

She pretended like she was cool but in the upcoming weeks, after the proposal didn't happen, it lead to a downward spiral of cutting herself and at one point attempting to jump out of my car as I was driving. That was the last straw.

This attention seeking crazy bitch did that shit because she felt I loved our child more than her. She was right but I didn't tell her that. I snatched her ass up promised to kill her if she ever harmed my baby. For fear of me leaving her kept her cool until the baby was born.

Once my daughter was here things kind of got back to normal. But of course with Leshaniqua shit could never stay sweet for too long before she showed her ass.

***

"Damn she sounds like a headache."

"Nothing but a headache. I even had to ban her from my restaurants. She has so much shit with her it ain't funny. So what's up with your relationship."

"I'll keep it short and simple. My man couldn't stay out of jail. We have three children and I just got fed up with being with a nigga who thinks jail is a revolving door."

I touched her face. Whoever that nigga was she was with had to be dumb as hell. Magic seemed like the type to be wifed up and spoiled. I may just have to move in and handle that position.

Both of us were comfortable on the sofa, she had snuggled close to me and we had got under a blanket just watching old movies like Higher Learning and Love and Basketball. Magic had said these were some of her favorites. She had fallen asleep. I was not too far behind her but my phone kept vibrating. I had quite a few missed calls and text messages from Leshaniqua. I read not one and deleted them all. I was sick of her ass and on to new better things.

Chapter 7 Eureka

I woke up to this nigga frying bacon and red link sausages, making breakfast naked like we were on Baby Boy or some shit. Still wearing the sexy negligee from last night, garters and all I walked into the kitchen with my ponytail all frizzy. I looked a hot ass mess this morning. Meanwhile this nigga looked like a black Adonis with his dick just swinging.

I didn't forget about his ass standing me up last night. As strong as that back looked and the way I could see that third leg hanging, I hope he does not think that all will be forgiven with this shit.

In any other instances, I would have loved to run up to him and grab and rub on that strong back of his but this morning that shit did absolutely nothing for me.

"Good morning, Eureka. You're up earlier than I expected. I was trying to make you breakfast in bed."

He turned around and I couldn't take my eyes off his dick.

"Good morning, Boo," I replied dry as hell. Last night I was wet for him and he had played me.

"Sit down and eat breakfast. I wanted to come over and make it up to you for last night." He pulled out my chair.

"Oh did you. What's your excuse this time for leaving me high and dry, better yet wet and ready? If you don't fuck with me that's all you gotta say."

He placed our plates on the table and sat down across from me.

"You know I fuck with you. I had some shit that came up. I'm sorry."

Damn right your ass is sorry. You were going to pay for fucking with me this was my breaking point with his ass.

"How long have you known you've had muscular atrophy in the hands?"

Boo looked at me all crazy.

"I'm just saying. I mean your fingers don't work as well as they should and it stops you from answering any of your phones. Do you know I called all of your phones Boo!"

He frowned up his face. "What you talkin' 'bout Reka?"

"It's gotta be something, most likely caused by muscle atrophy. That's the only explanation that makes any sense. If your fingers were working maybe you could answer calls, then maybe I wouldn't get so stressed. Maybe then would my blood pressure won't be sky high through the fucking roof! And then you want to serve me all this damn salty, fried pork!"

I took a big bite of the red link sausage that was split in the middle. Damn the hot grease ran down the side of my mouth. Mad or not the food was good. I didn't want to get distracted so I slammed my fist down on the table rattling the glass of juice. Boo had never seen me act like this before. He better shut up and listen.

"When you don't answer my calls, my mind can only go to one of four places, being the inevitable: you're either in jail, dead, or your hands are paralyzed." I laughed.

"That's only three things. What's the fourth? Your ass is crazy." He squinted his eyes at me.

"Now, you want to call me crazy when I called all of your phones, blew up your social media and you ain't answer. WHAT IN THE HELL HAVING YOU BEEN DOING BOO? Ducking and dodging me? But baby rest assured because two can play that game."

"I had no idea you were going trip like this. I fell asleep shit. When I woke up, I came straight over. Chill out damn."

All I wanted was to settle down and have a good man. I thought Boo was that good man. He was handsome, he had his own shit. He was the type of nigga I wanted to settle down with. Shit to me Boo was a rich nigga.

A rich nigga to me was one that was going hold shit down and just ride for me. I came from the hood so I always loved me a thug nigga one who had bossed the fuck up and had that shit in order. Boo was that nigga. I could never see myself with a square ass nigga. I wanted me a hood rich nigga, period pooh! All and all I was a good ass woman and he couldn't see it in me so it was time for me to move the hell on with this shit.

"You don't have to say shit Boo. Just go ahead and get out of my house. I tried to fuck with you and play by your rules but that ain't get me nowhere so I am done. You hear me I am done."

He must have thought I was joking. I grabbed his plate and flung it across the room. Eggs, bacon and sausage slid down the wall and the plate crashed to the floor into pieces.

"Get the fuck out of my house and my life nigga!"

"Reka you are tripping. All this shit ain't necessary. You got it. I'm out."

He stepped over the mess I made and exited my apartment.

I didn't need that nigga. He had me fucked up. All I wanted was to love up on a nigga who loved the fuck out of me and have a kid or two. I was never asking too much I think, I was just asking the wrong nigga.

Today was one of those days where I fell back on what I knew. If I didn't know how to do anything else I knew how to pray. I fell down on my knees and prayed about everything. By the time I was done my face was soaked in tears. I just wanted to be happy. I knew my prayer would not go unheard as I had.

Chapter 8 Magic

I've always wanted to get married on the beach. My wedding was perfect. I walked down the aisle to my man and nothing could be better. I was the happiest woman on earth walking down the aisle to Avant. When it was time to say I do it was Tom Tom instead.

My dream was over. I woke up immediately. When I looked around, I was not in my room I was in a king-sized bed in a room with a big tv across the wall. I noticed the French doors leading to a balcony. I was damn sure not at home. This massive bed and bedroom was twice the size of my own.

I was wearing nothing but a t-shirt and my panties. I walked out to the balcony and Avant was sitting out there with no shirt on with just pajama bottoms. Everything he wore looked damn good on him. That nigga even made sleep pants sexy. He looked fine as fuck sitting on the balcony.

"Good morning, Magic." He smiled at me.

"Good morning." I must have had way too much to drink last night. What the hell was I doing with my boss this morning? Yeah, we had fucked that one time but I had been doing everything I could to avoid going there again.

"Just so you know you don't have to work today. I'm giving you a few days off."

"I need my money I can't just take off."

"I'm the boss. And you are with me so you're good."

I didn't want him to be doing any special favors or shit for me just because we were talking or whatever the hell this was. I didn't want anyone to get to talking about me fucking with the boss either. I just didn't need any drama in my life.

"I'm going to handle some business and I just thought since it was out of town you could roll with me if that's cool."

"I would just have to let my kids' Aunt know what's up or whatever. I am sure she wouldn't mind."

Last night I had called Auntie Reba and told her I was staying out all night. She didn't seem to mind that I left the girls over there but I know that she was loyal to her family so she probably couldn't wait to talk to her nephew to tell him that.

"Do whatever it is you need to do. I got you for the next few days."

"Well let me call her and let me get dressed."

"We can swing by your spot and get some clothes and then we going hit the highway. We will be back sometime Friday. I got to finalize some stuff for some food trucks I'm going to be getting. I mean we going out of town but its work related."

"Shit I'm down for any kind of trip."

I hadn't really been anywhere especially since before I had Taymar and she would be three soon. If we went an hour away I was cool with that. All I had been doing before I started working was sitting my ass in the house. Tom Tom didn't want to take me anywhere or to do shit.

Avant had done his thing today while we were out. The food trucks he picked out would be delivered. He had paid for them cash. I didn't realize how caked up he was. I was right next to him as he was handling business. He had such a commanding presence to him. People around him knew he meant business and didn't play games.

I liked how he asked for my input and I could be myself around him. I had been smiling all day. I loved that he was a boss in every way. That turned me the fuck on, he had earned this pussy. Had we not talked the whole night before I would have given him the goods but it was better late than never. I had been thinking about that dick ever since the first time we had linked up.

The other night we had talked and fallen asleep but tonight none of that was taking place. We were going get straight down to business. We had just come from dinner. I could barely eat in anticipation for getting some more of that dick. I could've skipped the whole meal for real.

While at dinner he kept feeling my pussy making me so horny. He had felt me up in the elevator kissing me. I was so horny I would have given him the pussy right there in the elevator.

As soon as the doors opened I ran to our room and unlocked the hotel suite's door, and walked in first. The moment Avant was inside good and had shut the door, I leaped onto him. I pushed my mouth against his and immediately began tonguing him down continuing what he had started earlier. He placed both hands on my ass as we sucked faces.

I reached down to unbutton Avant's pants as his hands explored my body. When his pants had fallen to the floor, I broke our kiss and took a step back. I pulled off the dress I was wearing before getting down to my knees. His big, dick was in perfect height with my mouth. I couldn't wait to suck on it like a lollipop. It was rock hard. I immediately wrapped my thick lips around it and began sucking and gagging.

Avant let out moan after moan as I worked his dick in and out of my mouth, sucking it just hard enough to keep him from coming right away. After a few minutes, I noticed him leaning back against the door, closing his eyes and panting heavily.

"Damn Magic! Oh shit." He said in between moans.

Not wanting him to come just yet, I let his dick out of my mouth and stood up.

"Come on," I whispered as I started walking further into the room.

Avant was right behind me with his arms wrapped around my waist. I stopped to step out of my underwear giving him a full view of my pierced, chocolate nipples and my shaved pussy. I toyed with my hard nipples and licked my lips seductively.

"Fuck me," I begged, and gave Avant a tongue kiss.

I lay back on the bed and spread my legs apart using my hands. My pussy was bald, without a hair in sight. My excited clit and wet pussy lips were right there on display for him.

"I'm going fuck the shit out of that pretty pussy," Avant mumbled before getting himself into position.

He got in front of me and spread his legs to stand steady while grabbing my legs to pull them even further apart. He aimed his rock, hard dick at my pussy and thrust forward. He slid inside causing me to gasp, and he began moving his hips with power thrusts.

"Fuck, you're tight," Avant moaned as he begins to beat my back out.

I kept this Snapple nice and tight. I did Kegels all day and I had a low body count. I had been waiting on this moment to feel him inside of me again since the last time he fucked me silly.

Avant had started fucking me faster and faster, long dicking me. I felt my entire body moving up and down on the bed as Avant drove his dick deeper and deeper inside me with every thrust. He was making my juices flow nonstop. I creamed so much I was weak the way he was hitting my pussy.

His dick was just perfect for me. He rubbed right against my G-spot with almost every thrust.

"Yes, baby fuck this pussy!"

I reached down between my legs to rub my clit and felt myself being overtaken by pleasure ready to come again.

"Who pussy is this Magic?"

I rubbed my clit faster and faster as Avant kept hitting all the right spots inside me. I loved when a nigga talked to me while in that pussy.

"It's yours Avant. This your pussy! Oh, shit I'm ready to come again."

That was a benefit of having a tight pussy - it didn't take long for me to come. Before I knew it, I felt myself being flooded by wave after wave of pleasure. I let out a long scream as I tightened every muscle in my body and felt my thighs quiver. Avant showed no sign of stopping, making the pleasure even more intense for me as he beat my back out.

"Let that shit out! Get you another one."

As my body relaxed, I took a moment to look Avant in the eyes. He was a lot taller than me, and I loved how tiny I felt in comparison to him. He was looking right back at me while running his hands up and down my body.

Avant started slowing down before coming to a complete stop. I had just about regained my senses after my orgasm, but I could still feel my pussy pulsating around his dick. Avant pulled out. I guess he didn't want to come too soon. That was a side effect of grade A pussy.

"Ride me, Magic," Avant said, climbing onto the bed. "Sit on it," he commanded.

He laid on his back as far up the bed as he could get, with his head resting on one of the pillows. I obliged and I rolled around to my stomach and started crawling over toward him. I stopped with my face between his legs to give his dick a couple of wet sloppy, kisses before straddling Avant's lap. A nigga like him with money, that he was giving up; good dick, that he was serving, I was willing to be submissive all day, every day.

I stood up with my feet about midway down Avant's arms. I put my hands down on his strong body to support myself as I squatted down, making sure to keep my pussy just above his dick. When I was almost all the way down, Avant placed both of his hands on my ass cheeks and helped lift me. I smiled, before grabbing his dick between my legs and guiding it toward my wet pussy.

As I finally sat down on his dick and it slid inside me, I let out a gasp - partly to tease Avant a little, but also just because it felt so fucking good to be fucked by him. I had dick before but nothing like this in my life.

I started jumping up and down on his dick and Avant helped lift me.

My cowgirl technique was tried and true thanks to Tom Tom. He was the second nigga I'd ever fucked, but he was not the last. I had my secrets too. His lazy ass had good dick, but he didn't want to put in any work.

This nigga would just lift me onto his lap and expected me to do all the work. I'd just about managed to keep jumping up and down his dick long enough to make him come - but my thighs would be exhausted after the fact. I'd learned a couple of things from that. One - I would have to do squats, and two - if I knew I could handle the squats, why not start using squats as my dick riding-technique?

I used to just sit on Tom Tom's lap, just working my body forward. After doing all the work, I had tried my new technique. I started by standing over him and then crouching down, never sitting entirely. He had helped my lift my body up and down, and everything had turned out better. He had let out a loud roar after just a couple of minutes and blasted a massive load inside me, and my thighs hadn't been as tired as the time before. I know for a fact I had gotten knocked up both times dropping this good pussy down on that dick. My good pussy is what kept that nigga in check for so damn long.

The kind of squatting I had been practicing was perfect for dick riding. Thanks to the squats I could get all that good dick inside me. I was yet to meet a nigga who didn't love smashing balls deep.

Avant was no exception, and I was starting to feel his fat stick, deeper inside me with every thrust. He was still keeping his hands on my ass, and I twirled my hard nipples. I leaned forward so he could suck on them one by one. I loved that shit. That opened up the floodgates. I occasionally scratched his chest with my long fingernails - just lightly enough to hopefully make him want to fuck me a little harder.

"Fuck," Avant moaned after a while. "You so tight. I'm gonna bust a fat nut all in this pussy!"

I heard him, but I didn't really care that much. As far as I was concerned, he could come anywhere he wanted. I could happily keep riding him until he blasted all up inside me.

However, it seemed like Avant had other things in mind. He suddenly grabbed my hips and lifted me off his dick. I ended up lying on my back next to him, and I took the opportunity to give my clit some attention. It was beating like a heartbeat.

Avant hurried to kneel down next to me and I turned my face towards his dick, which he was aiming at my mouth. He didn't really seem to be aiming at my face, so I decided to wrap my lips around his dick and let my tongue flick around the underside of it, licking from the balls to the head making sure to make it sloppy and wet. I loved the taste of my own pussy on him. I could see why niggas loved to eat my juice box.

My licking seemed to be the last straw for Avant. He bucked his hips, let out a loud moan, "Oh shit Magic!!!"

He began shooting his load into my mouth. I felt his hard shots dance against the back of my throat and was tempted to swallow it right away. I ultimately decided against it, wanting to put on a little show.

The moment I felt his dick starting to soften, I opened my eyes and looked up at Avant. I pushed the come in my mouth out making bubbles. As if that wasn't enough, I took his dick out of my mouth and wiped it off against my chin, leaving a trace of come just big enough to spot.

When I felt finished with his dick, I sat up. Avant laid down on his back but didn't take his eyes off me. I smirked, opened my mouth and showed him the big load still left on my tongue, before closing my mouth and swallowing it all in one, big gulp. Once again, I opened my mouth and stuck my tongue out to show that the come was gone.

Avant smiled at my nasty little show, and I decided to snuggle up with him. I crawled over to him and rolled onto my stomach. This nigga had fucked the brakes off me now I was tired as a bitch. Avant wrapped an arm around me, letting his hand rest on my ass and giving it a light squeeze before we fell asleep.

This little road trip was much needed with Avant. I wasn't trying to rush into anything with him but shit was happening so fast.

"I'm not trying to rush into anything with you Avant."

He clutched my thigh as we rode up 95 North. The whole ride back this nigga had been loving on me and I was loving that shit. Last night had changed things with us.

"We don't gotta rush but you will be mine."

This nigga had me open and shit. I had never felt the way he was making me feel. I just looked at him and smiled.

He had gotten everything straight with the business and now we were going home.

When I arrived at Auntie Reba house to get my kids all hell broke loose. Tom Tom was standing by a black Hyundai Accent palming some girl's ass. She didn't look like too much of shit with her high cheekbones and chinky eyes. Her face with caked with makeup and she was dressed like she was ready to be in the next rap video. He was hugged up on her like he loved the fuck out of her. I didn't really give a fuck what he had going on honestly. I guess that pissed him off. He shoved the girl off of him.

"What the fuck you doing staying out all night and leaving my kids over here for Magic?" Tom Tom yelled.

I would be lying if I said he didn't look good standing there with a wife beater on showing off all his tats. His pretty eyes caught the right amount of sunlight. He had on jeans that hung low but still covering his ass, held up by a Hermes belt and some new wheat Timberlands.

I had got out of the car ignoring his ass. He was following me to the door. I continued to ignore his ass. He tried to grab my arm when I got to the top of the steps but I snatched away from him.

This high-pitched, annoying voiced thot had the audacity to yell out, "Tom Tom why are you tripping over that bitch for? You got all this woman right here. You don't need her." The girl had an up top accent.

"Alaina, bitch shut the fuck up. That's my wife don't you ever speak on her again." He roared at the girl.

"Fuck you Tom Tom. You weren't saying all that when I was riding your dick and you were busting all in this good pussy!"

I was not shocked nor surprised. I didn't have time for this circus.

"Nigga get away off me. You got what you want over there." I pointed at his bitch.

"Magic baby---" He was pleading.

I didn't want to hear shit he was saying I just wanted to get my kids and go home. Before I could do or say anything else Avant hopped out the car with his gun handle showing in the front of his jeans.

"You fucking with this bitch ass nigga Magic?"

Avant and Tom Tom stared each other down. Avant made sure to let Tom Tom know he was strapped. I didn't know what the fuck was about to happen.

The hood rat bitch that my baby daddy was with was thirsty as it could get. Her messy ass saw Avant and said, "Damn he is fine." I guess it was supposed to be under her breath but this hot pussy whore let it be known she was checking Avant.

When I pulled up to get the kids I got Avant to bring me. He drove his car with the dark tint. Tom Tom was so boo'd up he didn't even realize that I wasn't driving my own shit.

"Bitch shut the fuck up." I had heard enough from her non-factor ass.

"This ain't what you want nigga."

Avant had some thug in him as he mean mugged Tom Tom. This was new to me. The sight of him with that gun turned me the fuck on. I didn't have him being some bitch ass, weak ass nigga but he was standing toe to toe with my crazy ass baby daddy.

"You are going to have to see me about my wife and kids. You not about to be playing around with my family."

Tom Tom sounded dumb as a bitch.

"I knew you still had feelings for her. I have been riding for you and putting money on your books and you still in love with this bitch. I don't got time for this shit."

Alaina got in the Hyundai which I assumed was hers. The motherfucker sounded like she needed a tune-up as it struggled to crank. Once it finished struggling to start, she pulled off like a bat out of hell.

Auntie Reba came to the door after hearing all the commotion. Of course, we were in the hood so everyone was out here looking. This was the highlight of everyone's day. These bitches ain't have a life so this was prime entertainment.

"Tom Tom I told you don't bring this drama and shit to my fucking house! And what you do! You out here with this bald-headed hoe starting shit." She pointed in the direction of the black car making its way up the hill.

"I just want to get my kids that's it. I didn't come over here for no drama or this bullshit." I looked at Tom Tom. Auntie Reba knew that nigga was forever with the shit. I would never bring any drama to her doorstep.

"What the fuck is yall looking at it ain't nothing to see. Move the fuck along!"

Auntie Reba had cussed out the spectators and her one of her daughters, Sari was out there with her now doing the same thing. Sari went into the house to get the kids. I am so glad she was not messy like her cousin.

Avant stood close to me in case anything jumped off and held my hand. We got the kids and made it to the car. I put Taymar in her car seat and made sure Tommie was buckled up. Of course, Tom Tom was not about to let us ride off into the sunset.

"Magic you better look both ways before you cross me bitch!"

Avant wanted to get back out the car at those words.

"Baby it's all good. I'm not worried about his punk ass or his threats."

"You don't have to be as long as you are with me."

Chapter 9 Eureka

I hope I look good enough for my date. I finally agreed to go out with him for coffee. I mean what was the worst that could happen. I like coffee and I like his fine ass enough. As long as he wasn't trying to take me to a church event I was cool with going out with Deacon. He had been asking me out forever and I finally said yes. We met over two years ago at church. I immediately removed him from my dating list when my mother thought he was just the type of man I should be dating.

To keep my mother calm I had attended church with her Sunday. Before I could make my early departure she found every reason in the world for me to stay a little longer as she went back to get something. Her slick ass had probably conspired with this nigga. While waiting for her Deacon approached me in the lobby area.

His button up shirt could not hide those strong arms and his slacks fit his body just right. I'm always going be me so my eyes landed between his legs and I could see clear as day, even when he tried to hide it that the brother was working with something. I'm glad my mother was not standing right beside me because she would have pinched the shit out me or hit me with her purse the way I just moaned in approval in church!

"You are something else Eureka." Even the sound of his voice made me weak. Everything about this nigga was fine.

"Yeah I know!" I fanned myself. He was making me hot.

"It's good to see you here this Sunday." He grabbed my hand. *Me kissing him and throwing my legs around his waist would have been just too much for church.* The way these people around here talked him grabbing my hand was a bit too much.

"Yeah, well my mother promised me dinner today if I came so here I am." I noticed him looking over me in approval. I wore a simple dress with sandals. As much as I loved to get sexy my mother was not going for that in the house of the Lord so I kept it classy and sexy the same time. I couldn't hide my curves if I wanted.

"Cool. So what you doing later?" He rubbed his hands on his neat facial hair. Him doing that put all my focus on those lips of his. He was feeling me as much as I was feeling him.

"I don't know for real." It was the summer I was going find something to get into as soon as I was free with my mother.

"I got some things to do later today so you are off the hook but how about tomorrow around eleven we go for coffee."

I looked up at him. "Who said I like coffee? I may be busy."

"I'm tired of chasing you woman. Stop making this hard. I know that you love coffee and that you only work appointment only on Monday so put your address in my phone so I can pick you up. I am really trying to get to know you."

I noticed his smile. It was beautiful. He was not taking no for an answer and it was like he had mind control as I put my info in his phone. I knew my mother had been running her mouth about the coffee. We said our good byes and I stood there watching him walk away. Deacon was fine as hell and could have had any of these thirsty bitches in the church but he wanted me.

Before I could do anything stupid my mother walked over to me. I knew they had planned this all along.

“I’m glad to see you spending time with your future husband.”

“Ma stop playing. I know you sent him over here.”

“I sure did. You keep playing around you going be mad when he with one of these ungrateful, undeserving winches. Don’t be sitting back saying it could have been me.”

As we exited the building I got a good glimpse of some of the females she was talking about. A few stragglers were lingering around now after church trying to “pray their way, do some bible study or Sunday dinner invite” onto some new dick. These chicks were pathetic.

I knew more than anyone that church niggas could be dogs too. I had grew up in the church. That was one reason why I had kept my distance from Deacon.

“Well ma if it makes you happy we are going out tomorrow so chill. Don’t go out and start hiring a wedding planner just yet.”

We hugged and said our goodbyes. The next morning, I woke up early and in time enough to clean up real quick. My place was spotless but I loved for it to have that just cleaned scent. After that I pulled out a couple of outfits to figure out what I was wearing. After trying on a few things I was finally dressed.

My ass was stacked like some pancakes in my frayed denim shorts and a cute off the shoulder top. My hair was braided in some throwback Iverson feed-in braids that reached my ass, compliments of working in the salon. I was still kind of shocked that hairstyle had come back out with an update, so you know me I had to be up on shit. Of course, I was not leaving out of the house without my lashes and make up. I had doubled up on my lashes so they would be thick and I had a natural beat with subtle colors, I didn't want to do too much.

After getting cute, I waited patiently for Deacon to pick me up. I didn't know if that was a good idea or a bad idea because Boo had a key but I doubt that his ass would be popping up anytime soon after I checked him. Normally I would meet niggas on those far and few times when I went out because I didn't want everyone to know where I lived but this nigga went to the same church and I didn't think he would try no fuck shit.

True to his word Deacon arrived at eleven on the dot. I was surprised to see the rose and lily bouquet with red roses, pink roses and pink lilies in a pretty, clear vase that he handed me. He rubbed his hands together and licked his lips.

"You look beautiful Eureka. These are for you."

I blushed. I was not used to a nigga telling me that I looked beautiful and bringing flowers.

"Thanks and thanks for the flowers. You looking right good yourself."

I sniffed the pretty flowers and placed them on the cocktail table. Next, I stepped back to get an eyeful of him. This nigga always wore white like he was a damn angel that walked right out of heaven. As usual, he was dressed to impress wearing a polo shirt, white shorts, white sneakers and had two gold chains around his neck. As usual, his expensive but not overpowering cologne did something to me. We smiled at one another. I broke the silence. I quickly grabbed my purse before I pushed up on him.

"Let's go..."

I led the way so he could watch me throw my booty in a circle. When we got downstairs to his car I was shocked. I don't know why I was expecting him to be driving some regular, basic shit. Even though we went to the same church I had never seen his car because unlike my mother I dipped out before service ended so I didn't have to talk with anyone after church. I was very impressed to see he was driving a white Porsche Panamera, with white rims.

Like the gentleman he is Deacon opened my door for me.

"Come on, get in. You like how I'm rolling?" He smiled. "What you thought I was going pick you up in, a bucket or something."

Hell, I was not expecting this nice vehicle that had memory foam seats welcoming my ass.

"I really don't know what to expect," I said in a low voice.

He was whipping a foreign car and he came with flowers and opened my door. All we were doing was going to have some coffee. I can only imagine if we were going to dinner or something.

"With me expect the unexpected. In a good way."

He turned on the music and I was expecting to hear some Kirk Franklin or Mary Mary or whatever. He was listening to rap.

"You can turn to whatever you want to listen to."

He didn't have to tell me twice. I quickly turned to Megan Thee Stallion. He didn't seem to mind. He just drove. Meanwhile, I was giving him a whole concert on the passenger side, dancing, and rapping. We ended up going to this new black-owned coffee spot. Once we pulled up to the front of the building he got out and opened my door for me again. I could get used to this shit.

While seated at a booth we sipped on coffee and enjoyed goodies from the bakery. Everything was good, the food and the conversation.

I had given him the whole run down of my life and now it was his turn to tell his story as I listened attentively. I'm sorry that I had been giving this guy the run around he was really cool. I was surprised to find out that he was once a well-known drug dealer. Maybe that's how he could afford the luxury car he drove and that heavy jewelry on his neck and wrist.

"I'm glad that we could finally do this. Listen Eureka I am not trying to go to church but trust me I know what it's like to feel trapped in sin. I'm now a changed man and want those struggling to make a change to know God hears their prayers."

"I'm listening. This is a judgment free zone."

"I always try to tell people to look for the evidence of God because it's always there and sometimes we just ignore it. We look past it 'cause it doesn't look inviting to us," he said.

Just from listening to him I learned as a young child, Deacon's family attended church every Sunday and all services in between. He came from a family like mine, who lived in the church. His family relocated from Alabama to Virginia and his father, once a deacon and a member of the choir, became a mean, violent drunk who beat his mother daily and ran his household very strictly. After getting with another woman in the church and making their life a living hell his father abandoned the family leaving him to be the man of the house.

It hurt me to listen to him open up and tell me this. You never knew what people had been going through. I also learned that he had been living in the same city for years so it was crazy we had never crossed paths until we were grown.

As an adult, he became involved in illegal activities such as selling drugs and constantly faced the threat of jail or prison. Luckily he was never put in jail so he was able to turn his life around. Deacon is now a licensed counselor with his own non-profit organization, focused on breaking the cycle of poverty, and teaching men how to become better men for their children.

Deacon said he prayed five to ten times a day for the abuse to stop but it continued before his father finally left. He and two younger sisters Johnae and Rel eventually stopped praying. He had lost faith and begin to stray away from the church.

Then his family stopped attending church regularly and he said, "A couple of times I remember different ministers tried to reach out to us and my mom wouldn't talk to them. She said what goes on in this house stays in this house."

His mother also didn't allow them to talk to school counselors as far as their home life. People around knew things were not right with the family.

Deacon rebelled against God. He was kicked out of school by age 16. Both Johnae and Rel had both followed in his footsteps, in the streets. Their mother couldn't tell them anything. Rel eventually became a teen mother.

Deacon did not begin to seek God again until Johnae was killed outside of a party by a bullet meant for someone else. He cried out to God. It was from the death of his sister that he received a lump sum of money from insurance that afforded him his lifestyle. He couldn't get the money until he was twenty-five. This is when his life began to change for the better.

"God began to work in my life, freeing me of my drug and gambling addictions and providing salvation. Church took me out of the streets." Deacon says with confidence, "Jesus Christ is real."

All I could say was, "Wow." To be so young he had been through a lot.

I looked down at my bag beside me. My phone kept vibrating in my purse. I would get back whoever it was later because I didn't want to be rude.

"Yeah I've been through a lot but God has been good to me."

"Yes, he has been good to you, Jackson. So tell me why are you single?" A fine man like him had no problems getting a woman yet he was down on me.

"I have to make sure she is right for one. Women at especially at church love to try to date me or pair me up with someone."

"Oh, I know all about that," hinting at my mother. We both shared a laugh.

"Sometimes, I can't even talk to someone of the opposite sex without everyone wondering if they should get ready for a wedding."

"Stop being dramatic."

I enjoyed spending time with him because he had me feeling all kinds of emotions. I had almost shed a tear now he had me damn near crying, laughing.

"I think it's better for us to keep things discreet and on the low for as long as we can – but be prepared for people to figure it out pretty quickly!"

"One day at a time playboy. Who said we were a thing?" I made air quotations.

"Eventually we will be Eureka." I just loved the way he said my name. I was more into him now than ever especially since I knew he was not just some lame ass, church nigga. I should have known better all along, he always had a vibe to him and carried himself like he was that nigga. Nothing about Deacon said he wasn't a cornball or a fuck nigga. I guess I just had to get past the whole I love God thing. I was happy that we were both peeling back layers today and getting to know one another.

"Just being here today and asking you out for coffee is something like a proposal of marriage. You know that right?"

The waitress had refilled both our cups of coffee. I was envious of that cup the way he held it and put it to his lips. I had a proposal for him alright.

"Yep, three dates in and people start dropping hints about wedding bells. It's enough to put anyone off. There's often pressure, spoken or unspoke for people to marry quickly. My parents have been trying it, well my mother."

My mother knew I loved to party. She wanted me to sit the hell down and be a good wife or at least settle down. Partly to avoid sexual temptation, and partly because die-hard Christians like her live for marriage and family. But what my mommy didn't know was that she had put so much pressure on my even having a relationship.

I know that it's important to take my time and enjoy getting to know a potential love interest without feeling like I'm signing my life away this is why I preferred to just live life and do me. When the shit was supposed to happen it would. I was not about to force anything, my friendships, ponytails, or relationships.

Deacon interrupted my thoughts. “If people drop hints or ask directly about my dating life I simply explain that I take marriage far too seriously to rush into anything.”

“That makes sense. I’m just enjoying my life and doing me. It’s the summer so if a nigga wants me he better try again once it gets cold. For now, I am going to live my best life.”

“What you fail to realize is the best is yet to come. God is always in our lives but we pay no attention to it because we tend to pray for things and tell God exactly how we want it to be done. God will answer our prayers but He doesn't do it in the way we ask Him to and so we never see it and we see it later.”

I took a bite of the delicious homemade oatmeal cream pie and licked the cream off the side of my mouth. I wasn’t even trying to be seductive. He forced me to listen because he spoke with a purpose. I had been running around trying to force some shit with Boo and dealing with a few non-factors. After my last incident with Boo, I was determined not to play the fool for no niggas, so it was going to be whatever it was going to be.

"So you are saying God is always there and if people could realize that, then their faith would bring them out of their desperate situation?"

Deacon reached across the table to touch my hand.

"That is exactly what I am saying. I also want you to know God led me to you."

Even though he looked like he was serious all the time he had a silly side too. Now was my turn to laugh. God did not lead him to me.

"Really."

"Yeah, he told me that you needed a nigga like me in your life Eureka."

He smiled a little and waited on my response. I didn't have one. We had already been here for over an hour just talking. Even if we just sat and said nothing I was fine without because we were vibing.

"Anything is possible." I blushed.

I didn't want to ruin our date so I was ready to wrap it up. I would definitely be looking forward to the next one.

It was still early when dropped me off. Deacon agreed to walk me upstairs but that wasn't necessary.

"I really enjoyed spending time with you today Eureka. I hope we can do this again real soon."

I was being silly and gave him the pound with my fist. "You my dog, so we will. I had a nice time with you too."

Ignoring my pound, he reached over and gave me a warm embrace. I needed that. I felt so good in his arms when he wrapped his arms around me. To tell the truth, I didn't want to let him go because it felt just right. I leaned over and kissed him on the cheek. That cologne was doing something to me making me weak.

I got out and walked backward smiling and waving.

"Talk to you soon Jackson!" I blew him a kiss and watched him pull off.

I still had the whole day free. Still basking in the afterglow of a good date I walked over and smelled the flowers. One would have thought I had gotten some good dick the way I was glowing.

Chapter 10 Avant

Tap. Tap. Tap.

Something kept hitting the window. I was trying to watch a movie with Magic when I kept hearing the noise.

"Do you hear that Magic?"

"Naw baby I don't hear anything."

"Stay right here. I'll be right back."

I turned the tv down and went to the door leaving Magic on the chair. I didn't see anything. Then I spotted my crazy ass baby mama with a long sleeve, jean shirt and some white booty shorts on showing off her ass. Her short hair was all over her head and it didn't look like it had been combed. She begin to walk towards me with her ass cheeks bouncing like two basketballs. That's when I noticed her makeup streamed face and the shirt was opened showing her tight midsection, she didn't look like someone who had given birth at all. When she got closer I noticed she didn't have on a bra or anything.

What the fuck kind of shit was she on?

"Leshaniqua what the fuck are you doing? Why are you out here?"

She started laughing and her voice cracked.

"Baby I was waiting for you. I thought you would never come out here."

I was in no mood to play with her. I didn't want to call the law on her but her ass needed to go.

"You need to leave Leshaniqua."

She reached out and tried to touch my face and I stepped back.

"I'm not going anywhere. I should be here. This is my home."

"This is not your home and you need to leave."

"Oh I get it. You got that bitch up in there!" She looked over my shoulder.

I just looked at her. I didn't get her. When she was here she didn't want me now she was acting all pressed. I blocked her view and looked back at the door. I didn't need Magic coming out here.

Leshaniqua dropped her top to the ground revealing perfect c cups. I noticed the pierced nipples right away.

"This what you like ain't it!?! You like your bitches to have pierced titties! These the same tatas that you used to love! Suck them like you do that black bitch!" She pointed to the house and how the hell did she know Magic had pierced nipples?

I was at my wits end with her. Leshaniqua shook her chest in my face.

I pushed her away.

“Put your shirt on and get the fuck on.”

We ended up in a shouting match.

“I’m not going anywhere! Make me leave! I pierced my nipples since you love them on old girl!” She yelled through clenched teeth.

Magic came to the door.

“What you looking at you black bitch! This between me and my man!” Leshaniqua yelled.

Magic bolted out the door and came running towards us. Before I could stop her she had punched Leshaniqua in the nose making her head snap back. She was leaking. Blood dripped from her nose as she swung back at Magic who was easily winning the fight. Leshaniqua was fighting in shorts and no shoes hitting air. She didn’t have a shirt or anything on as Magic beat her like a drum and punched her like a punching bag. The only thing she managed to do was claw Magic only angering her making her punch her even harder.

Leshaniqua cried out, “Get this wild animal off me Avant.” The way Magic dragged her across the patio my plants crashed and some of the chairs were knocked over. Magic now had her pinned in between one of the wicker chairs and the table. Leshaniqua got in a few weak punches but they didn't faze Magic. That only made Magic beat her worse.

I should have been the bigger man and gotten Magic off her but the way this bitch had been stressing me after the break up I let Magic get her shit off. I smiled inwardly as my present and future rocked my past. After watching Magic stomp a mud hole in my baby mother's ass I finally stepped in between them and broke it up.

Leshaniqua looked like Rudolph with that red nose as she cried and her nose still leaked. This time I didn't have to tell her to leave. She grabbed that shirt off the ground and put it to her nose and ran through the yard with big titties and ass shaking everywhere.

"This shit ain't over! It ain't over!!!!!!"

I looked over at Magic who had her fist balled up like she was ready to beat my ass next.

"This ain't what I signed up for Avant. I swear I thought you were different. I expected some stupid shit like this from Tom Tom but never in a million years did I expect this from you!"

"Baby trust me I had no idea her crazy ass was out here. I don't want her. We have been over. I am trying to build with you and be with you. You are the woman I want."

I tried to get her to come in the house. Even though I lived in a nice neighborhood didn't mean the nosey ass neighbors wouldn't call the police.

Once in the house I noticed Magic grabbing her things.

"Magic I don't want you to leave."

I reached for her arm. I didn't want her to leave. She was right where she needed to be.

Chapter 11 Magic

This bitch had lost her fucking marbles. I didn't do drama with my own baby daddy and I was not about to let someone else's baby daddy stress me out. This crazy bitch had went and got her nipples pierced and was trying to show them to Avant. I had never seen any shit like that.

I had no choice but to warm her fucking head up. She was playing with the right one. Avant had tried everything in the world to persuade me to stay but after she popped up like that I took my ass home. I would catch up with him when I cooled off. What was supposed to turned into a chill night turned into damn fight night. I was too old to play these games.

Luckily the kids were with Auntie Reba so I didn't have to worry about them. I couldn't wait to take a shower and lay down.

When I flipped on the lights in my room Tom Tom crazy ass was sitting in the room. I don't know what the hell he was doing here. This night was just getting worse and worse by the minute.

"What the fuck you doing here? You got a lot of nerves bringing your ass round here Tom Tom." I put my hand on my hip and shook my head.

He stared me up and down before speaking. "Did you give that nigga my pussy tonight?"

"Nigga you ain't got not one piece of pussy in here! I don't have to explain shit to you. Where is your woman? Shouldn't you be in her bed or guts and not in my place?"

"Daddy is home where he is supposed to be."

He walked up to me and tried to feel me up. This nigga had been home for at least two weeks and he hadn't thought about coming home as he called it. I guess he had been shacking up with his bitch or whatever the hell he had been doing. So what the fuck did he want now. I guess it was trouble in paradise.

"This ain't your home. I'm glad you're here though. You can get all your shit for once and for all."

I had packed all his shit up and put it in the closet downstairs after I saw him with that pencil thin bitch that day. Had he been a day later this shit would have been straight in the garbage. I was removing all dead weight and cleaning all clutter from my life starting with him and his shit.

"That's cold Magic."

"The only thing cold is this relationship. That shit is cold. I used to have the hots for you but that shit is over. You left me hanging so many times and did your dirt and always expected me to be around."

"People who love one another go through things. What don't kill us makes us stronger. If you love me you would fight for us."

"Are you really serious right now. I've fought all I could fight and I am moving on."

He looked me over. "It looks like you've been fighting for real."

That stupid hoe Leshaniqua' s blood decorated my jeans.

"Mind your business," I snapped. His blood could be next if he kept fucking with me. I was sick of his shit.

"You done got real slick out your mouth I see. What you on some Hot Girl, women empowerment shit. Yall bitches listen to a couple of rap songs now you wanna talk that shit. You ain't bout that life Magic."

He didn't know me as well as he thought. His time with me was up. For him to notice my change was funny. He had changed too. Normally he would have been in here trying to fight me but I guess he had a new bitch taking up his time. I was not mad at her. She could have all these problems. I was good on all that shit.

"I am really tired and I want to get my shower and get in the bed."

"I'm not stopping you. Shit let me get in with you."

"That's dead. I'm going to bed. When I come back out this shower I want you out my damn house."

"Play hard Magic. Your ass will be back. This aint the first time you tried to break it off with me."

Oh baby it was my last time.

When I came out of the shower he was gone with his two black, Hefty bags of clothes. I knew his messy ass though, this was long from over. I was not going to spend too much time dwelling on it. Sleep found me as soon as my head hit the pillow.

Morning came quick as the sun peeked in my bedroom window. The birds were chirping and someone was banging down the door.

"Can I ever get some rest around this bitch!" My whole body ached as I stomped to the door. I was getting too old to be fighting. The sun was barely rising yet someone was knocking at my door like the damn police.

"Girl open this door! It's your bestie!" Eureka sang out.

Who dicked her down last night?

I swung the door open and she came in swinging her braids in one direction and her big booty the other. I did not have time for her shit this morning. I followed her to the sofa where she took a seat. She had a tray of coffee and some breakfast sandwiches. She was right on time with that as I reached for my cup of joe and pulled the food out the bag.

"So what do I owe the pleasure of you coming by here so early?"

She popped her nude colored lips.

"Since you don't answer your phone these days I figured I'd pull up. I wanted to check in on you that's all."

I know I looked like shit this morning. I hadn't even gotten a chance to brush my teeth or wash my face. Meanwhile she sat across from me looking cute.

"Fair enough. Girl I just been a little busy. I got so much shit to tell you."

I opened my breakfast sandwich and begin to much as she begin to give me the run down.

"So I kicked Boo ass to the curb and me and Deacon been talking. I finally gave him a chance." She smiled showing all her teeth.

I'm glad I was finished chewing my food. My mouth fell open in surprise before I started running it again.

"Ok. Boo ass was bad news. I'm glad you done with his ass. A nigga can have all his shit together and still not act right. His ass living proof. So what's up with Deacon?"

Eureka had been down on my ass about how much a dog Tom Tom was yet she continued to let Boo fuck the shit out of her literally and figuratively every chance he got. I was glad she had put that shit behind her.

"Well we just been vibing and he cool as hell. He is nothing like I thought. I really thought he was going be forcing that religious shit down my throat but its not like that. He just a young, fly nigga. He cool."

My girl was over there blushing and shit. She looked happy. I was glad to see that. She chewed on the side of her lip waiting on my response.

"So Magic you got some tea you need to be spilling. First of all you come to the door with no bonnet or scarf on. Your hair looks like a damn rats nest. You all scratched up and shit. You look like shit this morning. The hell you got going on?"

I tried to smooth my hair down and I touched my face and crossed my arm to try and cover the scratches where Leshaniqua's bitch ass had clawed me. That was all she did. I had kicked that hoe's ass.

"You don't miss shit do you?" I laughed.

"Nope. You have been my best friend since middle school. The first day of school when I couldn't find a seat at the lunch table and you let me sit with you. I know you like the back of my hand. Now tell me Magic, which bitch do I need to pull up on? Or was it a nigga? I got something in my bag for shit like this!"

Eureka grabbed her bag.

"I got this sis! Calm down. I got into a fight with---"

"What the fuck happened?" Eureka was no longer smiling as she waited for my answer popping her knuckles.

I was the one who talked shit and Eureka was the one who laid hands. This is how it had always been. Even though I never had a problem defending myself she never let me. She would beat up a bitch and ask questions later. We were getting older and I did not need my girl in jail for a nothing ass female who had nothing to lose but her Facebook or Instagram account.

"I got into a fight with Avant's baby mother. I dragged that hoe! Beat the shit out of her."

"Wait a minute? What? Not that smooth, suave ass nigga? He got baby mama drama? That bitch scratched you up like a damn cat! She put her hands on my black girl Magic! I'm beatin' her ass and you can't stop me."

When her mind was made up there was no changing it. All I could do is try to talk her out of it.

"I promise you she going get hers. We will catch her around. Tom Tom ass got out early as promised. I go to pick my kids up and he out there hugged up with a bitch. So you already know that shit with us is dead. He had the nerve to show up last night."

"You got a whole lot of shit going on. Both our lives a little hectic right now. So you working today or what? We gotta link up real soon. It's much needed."

"Naw I took some time off. Got a few things I need to handle."

"Oh yeah that's right. Perks of fucking the boss. Ayeeeee!!!"

"Girl shut up."

"Oh I get it. Do you shit. As long as them bills getting paid and shit do you. But dammit we doing us today. What I want you to do is bring your ass in the shop and get your hair done. I will pay for it. Somebody can hook it up."

I touched my hair. *Did it really look that bad?*

"Yes, it looks a fucking mess!"

I noticed her braids. Even though I was not found of them damn zig zag braids back in the day I had to admit her hair was laid. "Who did you hair? It looks really good. Looks tight but it looks beautiful." I reached over to touch her hair.

"This new stylist in the shop that braids. Yeah she did the damn thing. You just make sure that you come by before 2 so you can get in somebody's chair ok!"

"I will. Once I get right we going do happy hour or something. We goin have a good time."

"Bet. I'll see you later."

After seeing my girl to the door I got up and got moving. I was going to sleep in today but now I was motivated to get my ass up and get the day going. I decided that since I was getting my hair done today I may as well get my nails and feet done later too. I was going to be on my bad bitch shit so I figured may as well do a little self-care.

I ran my bath water and got in so I could soak. It was still early and I had time and I really needed that relaxation only an Epsom salt bath could bring. While having a little self-care I also would make sure my pussy was shaved or Naired. I needed the snatch and the rest of my body hair free because Avant was definitely going be eating the box later after he saw me later. I had tried that vajayjay wax shit and I was not fond of waxing my lady parts. I guess I was old school and still shaved or used hair remover.

As my luck would have it I didn't have any razors so I put the hair remover lotion on the spots that needed it such as under my arms and down below and walked around my room gathering my clothes as the tub filled up.

I had my day planned out. First stop, get my hair and nails done then do the most! I was going to hang out with my girl and have me a little fun. My girls had been in good hands with Auntie Reba and that gave their stanking ass daddy a chance to spend much needed time with them.

Sitting naked in the bathroom on the toilet, scrolling my phone, I decided to shoot Avant a message. Last night I had ran out after that fight but shit I was ready to talk about things now. I didn't want to fuck this relationship up so I did the grown up thing. I sent him a text message.

Good morning baby. I need to see you tonight. I'll see you at 10p

I wasn't waiting for or expecting a response right now as I wiped the lotion off my body good and sank in the tub of water. Today was going to be all about doing me and everything else could fall in place.

Chapter 12 Eureka

the next morning when Magic gets up she calls Eureka. She goes to get her hair done. she meets her at the shop she calls in to work. when eureka gets off they went to pick up kids at Auntie Reba they decide to hang out in the hood

Leshaniqua comes to salon to get hair done, Gets dragged at hood.

Starts dating Deacon. Has to tell Shine she cant fuck with him. Boo starts to come back around. Eureka starts walking daily to lose weight. Her and

Real hot girl shit
Yeah, I'm in my bag, but I'm in his too
And that's why every time you see me, I got some new shoes

The music was on blast in the hair salon thank goodness the stuffy ass owner was not here. Her sister Jaz had opened up shop and like me she didn't give any fucks. I had already done two weave installs and was ready to get to the third client. My booth was in the corner but I was fine with that too. When I first started working here I was complaining about it but now I didn't really care. Bitches would skip the other stylist and come to the corner to get their wigs smoked.

It was a vibe today. I feeling really good about myself as I rapped along to the music. I was on my hot girl ish, unbothered, no worries, having a good time and being the bad bitch I am.

Good energy. As soon as I heard the intro to the song I turned the fuck up.

“Eureka you have two more clients on the books for today.” Jaz was tapping on the Ipad. She did usually did appointments and worked as the receptionist.

“Yeah and they better be on time or their asses are short today. My girl Magic should be sliding through soon. She going get a blowout. Anyone of the stylist can do that for her. Put it down in the books for me. I’m adding it to my booth fees for the week.”

“Got it.” Jaz made not of it and went back to the front area.

Bianca wanted us to support the shop so if we could add styles to the booth fee to pay the stylists at a discounted price. It was never over $50. That was one of the reasons I kept my hair on point.

I had been on cloud nine since I had been talking to Deacon. He was a whole breath of fresh air. He kept a smile on my face and kept me in a good mood. I was still riding the wave of his positive vibes and was trying to rub that shit off on everyone else.

I worked quickly sewing the long hair down on my client's hair so I could get her on with her day and continued to listen to the music. We had listened to the whole Megan Fever album and partied like we were at a damn concert while I worked on her hair. Luckily the salon was not packed today and time was flying. No sooner than I was done with her Magic came walking through the doors.

"That's my bae! That's my bae." I yelled when she came over to me.

"Hey Eureka. So who is doing my hair."

"Since I'm free looks like I'll be doing it." I directed her to the shampoo area so we could get to work. After about a good two hours and then some I had her hair dropping. I had washed it, deep conditioned it and decided to go with the silk press. Her hair was so long it looked like weave. My girl was fine!!!

"Damn Eureka you got me right!"

She looked in the mirror. I was so pleased with the results that I was ready to hit the town. I had Jaz give my last two clients the option of going with another stylist or rescheduling with me this week. Either way I was out this bitch today. I grabbed my things and we got out of here.

We headed to my car. The last time we went out she had drove so I would do the driving today.

"I know you said you wanna hit the nail shop but I am ready to turn up."

"We can do that later shit. You ready to be a damn lush already. What you got in mind."

Before I could run down what I had in mind Magic's phone rang.

"Girl Auntie Reba want me to bring the girls some more clothes."

"Shit let's chill in the hood. I know you don't want to but shit its always some shit going on out there."

"Naw I'm game today. Take me to get the clothes and lets pull up. I'm on all bullshit today."

"That's what I'm talking about. Grab one or two of them bottles when you go in there for the road."

We made the detour to Magic's house to get the stuff and headed across town. Just like any other summer time fine day the hood was beating when we pulled up.

Everyone was outside, the basketball court was packed, kids were outside. The young, old, the miserable and the messy were all in their respective places waiting to see what was going to jump off. We were not in the house a good twenty minutes before Auntie Reba and her daughter Sari decided to take the action to the front yard area. Sari was a cute petite chick and she had the family trademark of hazel eyes. Fine as she was she could have had any nigga she wanted but for some reason she was always sticking with her mother. A bad bitch like her definitely should have been riding the hot girl summer wave.

"Yall let's go outside. I'mma send somebody over to the crab lady house to get some crabs. What yall want fried or steamed? Never mind I'll get both." Auntie pulled a knot of money out her bra.

Meanwhile, Magic pulled the two bottles of liquor out her bag and Sari pulled out a big bag of smoke out her bag. We were ready to get the party started. We sat at an extended folding table yet still had a good view of the hood.

While they did all that talking I wasted no time rolling up. I was ready for all bald head hoe activities. Before long we were all smoking and drinking and having a good time. It was still a good two hours before the kids came from daycare and even when they did they were going in the house with the big kids so the grown ups could do their thing.

Auntie Reba broke the silence of everyone smoking and drinking.

"So Magic what's the deal with you and nephew. Keep it one hundred with me. Don't sugar coat shit."

I was all ears for this. I pulled the fuck out the blunt and looked back and forth.

"We done. He made his bed and now he gotta sleep in it. Whatever he got going on with scarecrow skeleton that's on his ass. I can't keep fucking with a nigga who won't stay out of jail."

Sari spoke up with her baby voice. "Girl I felt that. Cousin or not don't nobody got time for that shit."

"I just wanted to make sure you wasn't out here being stupid for him that's all."

Damn she gave no fucks about her nephew. Tom Tom's family must have been fed up with his shit. I guess everyone had enough of his shit.

"Naw he with that girl so he better make the best of it. He had me sending him money and not wanting me to work but the entire time he had his shit going on."

Speak of the mother fucking devil. The skinny bitch was walking up the steps leading to the front yard area. All eyes were on her. She walked up like twisting her bony ass hips before putting her hands over her eyes.

"Sari. Auntie. Yall seen Tom two times?"

Auntie Reba was rude as hell. "Girl that's your man ain't it? You lay with him at night don't come up here asking where he at? You keep tabs on his ass not us now gone head." She dismissed the girl.

She looked at all of us. Sari rolled her eyes at the girl. I looked at Magic. If my bitch wanted to stomp her ass out I was with it. All she had to do was blink and I was going set it off. Of all the bitches Tom Tom could fuck with he went got with his bitch. She was notorious in the hood for taking care of niggas. She would raise the fuck out a nigga before she took care of those three kids that didn't have fathers. For the life of me I was still trying to figure out how the hell she had landed a job at the regional jail. They must have had a shortage of staff or she fucked her way into the position.

This bitch was standing here looking stupid. The best thing to do was for her to carry her ass on. Since she wanted to stand there looking dumb I decided to fuck with her.

"Girl don't nobody call that nigga Tom two times but your slow ass. Guess there is trouble in paradise huh? What zaddy ain't come home last night?"

She stood in place looking like she was about to cry. Alaina tried to be bad with certain bitches but she knew this was not the move here. This ain't what she wanted.

"Naw he didn't. And he took my car."

"Sorry to hear that. So Auntie you got any more juice?" I yelled over the music. There was a Beats speaker beside the table playing hole in the wall ass music like Mel Waiters Got My Whisky.

The boy had arrived with the crabs and Alaina ass was dismissed. She wanted to take someone nigga take all the damn problems. We were trying to have a good time.

Magic was over there dying laughing the whole time. She was not thinking about that girl or her baby daddy for that matter an that was good to see. Shit she had that fine paid nigga so I guess she was unbothered. I was so happy to see her out that funk she had been in fucking with Tom Tom raggedy ass.

A candy apple red Yukon sitting on thirty inch rims pulled up and some short nigga jumped out. He had to be about five feet tall but from the looks of that new ass truck , the rims and the ice around his neck his mother fucking pockets was tall, deep and long.

He came up the steps and walked up to Sari. Oh shit now I aint know Sari was doing it like that. Its always them quiet ones.

"Baby you ready to roll?" He tongued her down and she wrapped her arms around his neck. All the nosey bitches on the court was looking. He was a short nigga but he was cute. A little rugged and cute. Him and Sari made a cute ass couple. He was light bright, damn near white with a tattoo over his right eye.

"Yeah let me grab my bag and I'm coming."

He went back to the truck and waited as she grabbed her stuff. When she came back out we had to shoot the shit.

Magic was first. "Damn Sari. I see you boo. He's a good look for you."

"Yeah girl that's bae. We bout to go out of town for a couple of days. I'm going catch yall girls when I come back."

Next I fucked with her. "Don't come back pregnant. I mean yall would make some pretty babies and shit."

"She better not bring no kids up in here. I don't have the time or room for no more kids in this spot." Auntie Reba said. She knew damn well if her baby had a baby she would be adding that baby to the rest of her fifty million kids she spoiled.

"Naw yall I'm doing online school to get my masters and shit. I don't got time. Don't have too much fun without me."

She jumped in the truck with her nigga and rolled off into the sunset.

"When I was yall age I ain't let no grass grow under my damn feet. I don't care what yall girls do but don't let no niggas try to get over on you." Auntie Reba was kicking real knowledge with that. At this point I was not about to play with these niggas.

My damn phone kept vibrating in my damn bag. Whoever the fuck it was had better wanted something. I had to use a bunch of paper towels and wet wipes to clean my hands before retrieving the phone out the bottom of my bag. I had started eating on the steamed crabs and now sipping on them low alcohol ass wine coolers. To get some buzz I had to pour some vodka with that shit.

I looked at my phone and it was the nigga Shine. I don't know what that married nigga wanted but all he could do for me was give me his money. I had been telling him time after time that's all he could do for me. He knew he was wrong for trying to holla at me but like I said I was not going turn down no money. I gu ess because he had sent me $500 via Cash App that I was supposed to jump. Well guess what I was. I was going jump right on that dick that he had been promising to fuck the shit out of me with for the longest. I didn't want his ass but I was going get all this damn money.

"What the hell you over there smiling at Eureka?" Magic raised her eyebrows at me. She had a nerve. She had just gotten off the phone with Avant so I already know she was ready to pull off at any minute.

"Damn you nosey. Deacon hit me up shit. He talking about bible study and shit later. Do you want to go?"

She didn't need to know my every move. I didn't want her saying shit about me deciding to fuck Shine. Didn't want her fucking that up for me. My rent was due soon and it was free money.

"Hell naw I don't want to go. Yall have fun. Pray for me while you are there. Shit what time we leaving anyway. I'm going get you to drop me off at Avant's place?"

Auntie Reba was messing with her phone to change the music but she didn't miss a beat.

"Magic you or your baby daddy getting yall kids this weekend. I said would watch them not adopt them. Auntie has to get her groove on too damn." She laughed.

"I'm getting the girls this weekend. You know Tom Tom ain't getting no kids. I love you Auntie." Magic hugged her. "Thanks for all that you do for us."

Being that there is always the quiet before the storm the bottom fell out. Tom Tom pulled up on that girl car fast as a bitch. He barely stopped it like the brakes were missing. He walked up dressed in a wife beater and khakis with Timbs on. Don't know who the hell he thought he was but the moment he trotted his ass up the stairs I know he was ready to come for Magic.

"Fuck you doing over here at my people house Magic. Your ass need to scram. Matter fact you don't need to be leaving here without your kids!" He pointed at her.

"Nigga who the fuck you talking to?" She yelled. "Get that raggedy ass finger out my face."

"Mane Tom Tom go head." He was not about to be talking to my girl any kind of way. I made my way closer to her.

He tried to push on Magic. If we didn't know before it was confirmed today that he had been beating her ass the way she cowered. Before I could do anything Auntie Reba checked his ass.

"Of all the dog ass shit you been doing I just know you ain't been putting your hands on this girl. Get the fuck from my house with this shit. I done told you before don't bring that hot shit over here. You need to leave."

He knew she didn't play with his ass. It was no point or use in trying to argue with her. Just as fast as he came up in the yard he was back in that bucket pulling off. His stupid ass just had to give the hood some shit to talk about. Being the bad bitches we were, we kept our heads up and left. Me and my best bitch were going to have a long ass conversation. I know we were supposed to be hot girls but this shit here was a hot ass mess.

Chapter 13 Eureka

A couple months later

The honeymoon was over and we were still going strong. Even though I said I was not going to rush into anything that is exactly what happened. Me and Avant had fucked around and gotten married without telling anyone. We had a beach wedding I had always dreamed about.

Now we were back home and everything was perfect. Avant was the kind of nigga I had always dreamed of. Shit was going beautiful and he had also stepped up to be the father my girls needed. I was happy with every aspect of my life the only thing missing was my girl Eureka. Her ass had been laying low. This was very unlike her. I was so busy with my man but I always had time for my best friend. When she called me today I was more than happy to hear from her.

"Magic!!!" She sang into the phone.

"Bitch where the fuck you been? Damn, I thought I was going to have to put a missing person report on your ass."

"I've just been cooling it for real sis. Making some changes. Everybody can't be loving on a rich nigga like you!"

"Bitch stop. I had no idea this shit was going to go this far. My husband is everything."

"Congrats and I am so happy for you. I can't wait to see you and my little boos."

"Where the hell you at or been?"

"Long story short remember Boo kept telling me to lose weight and all this other shit. Well, I been on my shit. I look the fuck good too. But that ain't all."

"I don't like surprises Eureka damn!"

"You will see tomorrow. Make sure to send me your new address."

I sent her the address after ending the call. My best friend sounded good. The last time we talked she was all fucked up about Boo and had started talking to that nigga from the church. I was glad she was able to take some time out to get her mind and body right.

I was getting my shit right too. The whole time I had been with Tom Tom I had never worked and I was a stay at home wife. Let me run that back again I had never been married but that nigga called me his wife. I had never gotten a job because he took care of me with his money. Now I was a real wife to Avant and he took care of me in every way. That nigga had bossed me the fuck up. I wasn't staying at home for shit.

I had enrolled in school to school to get my degree in Business Management and I was managing his restaurants. I didn't just want to sit around the house all day I had been there and done that. I was loving my new redirection in life.

After going to class all day I was at home studying in the living room when Eureka called me. I was not expecting the kids home for another hour or two when Avant picked them up from daycare on his way in.

"You living real good up in here I see! This is supposed to be my life!"

"What the fuck are you talking about! Get out of my house!" I yelled. I couldn't believe this was happening like this.

"This was supposed to be my life!"

I put my hands up in front of my eyes and tried to duck the blow that was coming and that was the last thing I heard before everything faded to black and I fell to the floor in a loud thud.

IF YOU HAVE QUESTIONS, COMMENTS OR CONCERNS PLEASE STAY TUNED FOR PART 2. FOLLOW THE AUTHOR FOR UPCOMING BOOK DISCUSSION AS WELL

IF YOU ENJOYED THIS BOOK PLEASE LEAVE A REVIEW ON AMAZON! SHARE THIS BOOK WITH OTHERS!!!

THANKS,

PEN N PAPER

Coming 2019

So Amazing Publications Presents
Loving A Boss
A Hot Girl Summer Story 2
PEN N PAPER

FOR THOSE LOOKING TO WRITE A BOOK

CHECK OUT MY BEST SELLER ON AMAZON

#1 NEW RELEASE

Guide to self-publishing Urban Fiction

Publish your book in 30 days

Become a bestselling author

Earn great royalties

Referrals to best Promoters and Graphic Designers on FB

So much more!!!

MAKE SURE TO CHECK OUT BOOKS BY MY PEN SISTER

<u>SERENITY JAMES</u>

AVAILABLE ON AMAZON

Serenity James